Anna's Town

Anna's Town

ROBERT COLEMAN

ANNA'S TOWN

Certain characters in this work are historical figures, and certain events portrayed did take place. However, this is a work of fiction. All of the other characters, names, and events as well as all places, incidents, organizations, and dialogue in this novel are either the products of the author's imagination or are used fictitiously.

iUniverse books may be ordered through booksellers or by contacting:

iUniverse
1663 Liberty Drive
Bloomington, IN 47403
www.iuniverse.com
1-800-Authors (1-800-288-4677)

Because of the dynamic nature of the Internet, any web addresses or links contained in this book may have changed since publication and may no longer be valid. The views expressed in this work are solely those of the author and do not necessarily reflect the views of the publisher, and the publisher hereby disclaims any responsibility for them.

ISBN: 978-1-5320-6963-5 (sc)
ISBN: 978-1-5320-6964-2 (e)

Library of Congress Control Number: 2019902242

Print information available on the last page.

iUniverse rev. date: 02/25/2019

To Maxine of course

You're the rock that anchors me
My shelter from the storms
And I believe that loving you
Is what God made me for

{From my notebook} RC

1

Pappy Moves The Family to Tupelo

PAPPY MOVED MY MOMMA, my brother, Willy, and me to Tupelo, in the fall of 1952, the day after Thanksgiving. We had been living with my Grandpa in his old house in Big Flat, and Pappy was farming a piece of land in the Potlocona River bottoms that we rented on the share from Mr. Joe Parker. My daddy owned his own plow tools, a pair of good Georgia mules and a nice New Holland wagon with a spring seat. Pappy paid Mr. Parker a quarter of the crop for the use of the land. Mr. Parker hadn't gotten much rent over the past three years, for we had seen three years of mighty poor crops. Mr. Parker was not real happy about that, but he was not nearly as upset as Pappy was. The river had flooded in late June for three years in a row, and had drowned the entirety of our corn crop, and a big portion of our cotton. By the time the water had receded, it was too late to replant. We were left with little showing, for a lot of hard work. It was a depressing time for us all, for I had never known a harder working man than my Pappy.

When we had finished scrapping up the last bale of cotton, Pappy loaded it onto our old 1940 Chevrolet Pickup, and took it to Pontotoc to be ginned and sold. He told us that night at the supper table that he did not have enough money to start a new crop and pay off what he had borrowed to make the last one, so he had sold his plow tools, as well as his team of Georgia mules and his New Holland wagon to pay out of debt. He was going to go to work in Tupelo for Mr. Wayne Purnell at his lumber yard. Momma never spoke a word till my daddy had finished talking but it was plain that she was filled with sorrow. Momma and Pappy had lived in Big Flat their whole lives, so it was sure enough hard to just up and leave a place after all that time, even though Big Flat was nothing but a wide spot in the road. Some folks were even willing to argue the wide part of that. I think it was not being able to make a go at farming that hurt Pappy the most for he truly loved being a farmer. But Pappy said everything always worked out for the best and that there was a purpose for everything under the sun. We sure couldn't see the truth of it all at the time though.

When Pappy had finished telling us his decision, he hung his head for a moment before he continued. We could all tell that Pappy was as sad as our mother about the situation. Grandpa sat at the other end of the table from my Pappy silent as a stone, sipping a cup of hot coffee. Grandpa was old; I guess in his seventies. He was a tall and lean man, with a wide handlebar moustache and thinning grey hair. Grandpa owned one of the two stores in Big Flat along with his brother Otto. The store business in Big Flat was nothing to brag about, but grandpa managed to get by. Grandma had died sometime back and I wondered what grandpa would do if we just left him.

"Is grandpa going with us?" I asked.

Momma just looked at me with her lips pressed tight together, tears glistening in her eyes, with a look that said more than I wanted to hear. But it was my daddy that answered.

"No, son. Grandpa will not be moving with us, but he's gonna be alright," he told me. "Aunt Zula, your grandpa's sister that lives in Atlanta, will be coming to stay with your grandpa for a while. Her husband died about a year ago, and she will take good care of your grandpa. They will be good company to each other, and we'll be coming back real often to see them."

Of course, I had heard of Atlanta from school, but I had never heard much positive of people from Georgia, so I was not exactly sure if this was a good development or not. It was plain that grandpa did not want my Pappy to move from the old house, but he knew the deal was already struck, and no amount of talk was going to change Pappy's mind after he'd given his word to Mr. Purnell. Pappy always said that a man's word was his bond, and you must never go back on your word for any reason. That philosophy, I have long since learned, is one that many folks subscribe to but mighty few actually practice.

Finally, Grandpa said, "AC, you take one of them hams, and a side of bacon from the smoke house, and whatever else you need in the way of canned goods."

Grandpa then got up and left the table. Moments later, we could hear his footfalls in the hallway, the creaking of the back door opening, and then closing, and finally the squeak of the old rocker on the back porch, and we knew grandpa was out there smoking his pipe of Velvet tobacco, staring out into the darkness. Pappy told Willy and me to get all our stuff together, for we would be loading the truck the next day for the move to Tupelo.

"I've got to be ready to go to work at the lumber yard on Monday," he had said to us.

I had never heard of Mr. Purnell before that night, but my pappy knew him from way back, and so did my mother. Pappy said he was a good man, and that they were in the war together, and that he had made a lot of money in the lumber business, and had offered him a job at fair wages. Fair wages meant sixty-five cents an hour. Pappy said he would be off work on Wednesday afternoons and Sundays, and would get seventy-five cents an hour for his Saturday work. He said Mr. Purnell would also furnish us with a house to live in that was close to the lumber yard until we could afford something of our own. Pappy said that if everything worked out, we'd have enough money saved in a year or two to get back in the farming business, and we'd be able to move back to Big Flat. Even at our young ages though, Willy and I knew that probably would not happen.

My brother, Willy, was fifteen years old and was in the ninth grade. He was nearing six foot. Willy was thin, and much like Pappy, he had a muscular build, with coal black hair and blue eyes. I was thirteen at the time, and had just started the seventh grade at Big Flat School. Everyone said I was my brother's look-a-like. Some even thought we were twins. We were both green as gourds though, and had never been more than fifty miles from Big Flat. We could see the old building where we went to school from our grandpa's place. It was a two story, wood frame building, with four classrooms and an office on the first floor, and two classrooms, an office, and an auditorium on the second floor. It wasn't much of a place, as far as schools go, but it was all we knew, and we were awfully sad about having to leave it behind.

While it was sad to be leaveing Big Flat, moving to a city like Tupelo was like a big adventure, and it was exciting in a way. Willy and I didn't sleep much that night, for we lay awake, deep into the night, and talked in whispers about what it would be like at our new home. We slept together in an old, iron bed in a room at the end of the big house that Momma just called the "side room". Hearing our whispers, Momma came in after a while, sat down on the side of the bed, and turned the lamp on. She seemed to me to know of our concern, and she hugged us both, telling us that everything would be just fine. Mommas like to hug you, even when you're thirteen. She said Pappy would see to it that we were all okay.

"Your daddy is doing what he thinks is best for all of us," she said. "Now you boys go to sleep, and be ready to go to your new home tomorrow. This was a very difficult decision for your daddy to make, but he feels it is what he has to do for the good of the whole family. I believe that each of us has a guardian angel, watching over us, she added, and he intervenes sometimes when we need his help if we ask. I think he is watching over us now. He will watch over both of you."

Momma stood up, turned out the light, and left the room, leaving Willy and me alone. However, it was a long time before we slept.

2

Saying Goodbye to Big Flat

THE NEXT MORNING, MOMMA woke us up just as it was beginning to turn light outside. Pappy had hired my uncle, Herman Epps, who owned a big flatbed truck, to move all the large heavy items such as Momma's Hoosier Cabinet, our table and chairs, and bedroom furniture. He, grandpa, and Uncle Herman had the big truck nearly loaded by the time Momma got us out of bed. Pappy said we would load the boxes of dishes and pictures and such on the old pickup truck. Pappy had already backed the old truck up to the porch to be loaded.

My mother fixed my brother Willy and me some breakfast, and we sat and ate in silence, both of us realizing that this would be our last meal in the old house for a long time. We had eaten every meal of our lives at the same, old table. As I ate, I remembered all the great times, and all the talks, that went on when we would all sit down and eat together. By the time we had finished, Pappy and grandpa had finished loading up most of the essentials that we were taking with us.

My brother and I didn't have many possessions, but the previous Christmas, Pappy had gotten each of us a Stan The Man autographed fielders glove, and two Louisville Slugger baseball bats. Pappy was a big Cardinal baseball fan, and we would listen to the games on the radio some nights after we had eaten supper and finished in the fields. We threw our personal belongings into the old rucksack that uncle Clint had brought home after the war, and loaded it onto the old truck before helping load other things for Pappy.

We had been loading the truck but a little while, when my uncle Bud and aunt Wilma crossed the gravel road to help us, and to say goodbye to Momma and Pappy. There were very few secrets in Big Flat, so everybody had already heard that we were leaving. Aunt Wilma hugged Momma, and they both cried for a bit. They went inside together, and began cleaning the old house. Momma said she wanted to leave the place clean for aunt Zula, but we suspected it was just a way to postpone the leaving for just a while longer, for Momma always kept our house mighty clean.

By the time the truck was loaded, the front yard was filled with kinfolk, neighbors and friends who had come to say goodbye and wish Momma and Pappy well. I wondered how the word got around so fast that we were moving. Willy just said that he guessed word traveled fast in a small town. There was a lot of hugging, and misty eyes all around, before we finally climbed into the old truck, and pulled out into the gravel road, leaving all of the other folks standing in the yard, waving goodbye.

We took the road from Big Flat, out past the schoolhouse and the Baptist Church, and up the big hill out of the little settlement. My brother and I looked out the back window, watching Big Flat disappear into the distance through the trail of dust left by the old truck. When we topped the hill, we drove along the ridge for a half mile or so, and we could see the Yocona River bottom before us on the left, and Big Flat in the valley on the right.

Soon, we left the ridge, and started down into the river bottom, passing fields of cotton and corn along the road. Most of the crops had been gathered, but there were a few pickers here and there, and Pappy would raise his hand high above the truck cab to wave at them as we drove by. They would wave back, for everyone around Big Flat knew Pappy's old truck. We crossed over the river bridge, hitting the Dogtown Road with the sun high, and sunshine coming through the front windshield. Two miles further on, we turned onto the Shiloh Cutoff Road passing by the old church and cemetery where many of our kinfolk were buried, and over to the state highway that would take us to Pontotoc, and then finally on to Tupelo, and our new home.

3

Stopover at Ponotoc

PAPPY STOPPED AT THE crossroads in Pontotoc, to get gas for the truck. The old man there pumped eight gallons for us, and a younger man in a Texaco uniform cleaned the windows, and then checked the oil and water for us while the gas was draining into the tank of Pappy's old truck.

An old, black man sat on an empty nail keg, rolling a cigarette from a tobacco sack that he had pulled from his shirt pocket. His hair was gray, and his face was lined with deep wrinkles. He cupped the white tobacco paper between his thumb and forefinger as he poured in a pinch of brown tobacco. With his other hand, he used his thumb and forefinger to roll the paper tightly. He held the rolled cigarette to his lips, then licked the seam with his tongue, before finally puting the end of the rolled cigarette between his lips to smoke. He took a match for the bib pocket of his overalls, flicked it with his thumb until it flamed, and lit the cigarette. He inhaled deeply, then blew out a large puff of smoke into the air. The smoking man saw that I was watching him, and he grinned big, showing that he was missing several teeth, but he never spoke a word. He looked as if he was enjoying the cigarette, but I couldn't see how, for I had tried smoking one of Pappy's Camel Cigarettes once, and it was about the worst experience I had ever had. I nearabout died from it.

The whites of the man's eyes were slightly clouded, and etched with deep, red veins. A hand-hewn walking cane was propped against his frail legs. A cardboard suitcase sat beside him, with nothing but a wide belt buckled around it to hold it together. His suitcase had a big, white tag tied to the handle, with "Memphis," stamped across it in red letters. Judging by the scene before me, and the signs around the place, I could tell that the service station also served as a bus stop.

Pontotoc was not a very large place, but compared to Big Flat, it was a metropolis. There was a lot of activity along the main highway, for it was late into the harvest season, and farmers were bringing their crops into town to sell. The familiar smell of freshly picked cotton permeated the air, and was inescapable.

Willy and I sat on a bench just outside the service station door, and watched with interest as pickup trucks passed in front of us, loaded up with cotton. In Big Flat, there was little traffic at any time. If you were going to watch traffic passing through Big Flat, you better bring lunch, and a dinner bucket, too, because you might be waiting a while. Thinking of lunch made my stomach rumble. The service station had a lunch counter, where waiting passengers could order coffee, sandwiches, and other items, but Pappy had told us not to go inside. We had no money to buy anything anyway.

It wasn't long before a large passenger bus pulled into the station, taking up all the station parking lot, and a chunk of the highway. A cloud of diesel smoke followed the bus as it rolled to a stop. The driver set the air brakes, and I nearbout jumped out of my skin, and took off running at the noise of the air being released. The driver climbed down out of the cab, took the black man's suitcase, and stowed it in a compartment underneath the bus. Not a single person stepped off the bus, and nobody else got on.

"Is that all the luggage you've got, boy?" the driver asked, never looking directly at the old man as he punched his ticket.

"All's I own in dis whole world is right here in this little satchel, sir," the black man told him. "I'd appreciate it very much if you'd take mighty good care of it for me."

The driver handed the old man back his punched ticket. "You can get on the bus now," was all he said to him as he walked into the service station.

The old man ambled his way up the steps of the bus and down the aisle to the very back seat of the bus. The driver came out of the station, climbed back into the cab, pulled the big side door closed, released the air brakes, and the bus roared away in a cloud of pungent grey smoke.

I could see the old man looking out the back window of the bus, propped up on his cane, as he disappeared through the dust and smoke into the distance. I watched the bus from the back of Pappy's truck until its tail lights were out of our sight. I wondered, though, why the old man was going to a city like Memphis.

4

The Crapper

PAPPY TOLD WILLY TO take me to the toilet around the backside of the service station. I thought it was odd that Pappy would tell him to take me, but I followed Willy to the door that said "restroom". Below the sign was a second sign that read, "FOR WHITES ONLY". I wondered aloud where the colored people went when they had to go.

"How the heck would I know?" Willy replied. "Hell, they may be like camels. Camels can go weeks without water, and don't have to piss for a month."

"How do you know so much about camels?" I asked him. "I bet you ain't never even seen a Camel in your whole life."

"No, I ain't never seen a real camel. I don't know nothing about camels, and I don't know nothing about colored people either," he said, getting short with me. "Sometimes you just ask way too many questions."

"I'm gonna tell Pappy you been cussin. He's gonna whip your butt."

"No you ain't gonna tell him nothing, 'cause then I'd tell him you been cussin' too, and he'd whip both our butts," Willy said.

"Then you'd be lying."

"I'd tell him that you're lying."

I didn't say anything else to my brother. There was no point.

Inside the restroom was a sink, and something that I did know what it was. Back in Big Flat, we only had outdoor toilets, even at the school. They didn't smell like no flower shop either.

"What to heck is that thing?" I asked my brother.

"It's called a commode, dummy," He said. "Pappa calls it a crapper, but I don't reckon he'd want you to be calling it that."

"Why does he calls it a crapper?" I asked him.

"Now, why do you reckon?"

"How to heck would I know?"

"Cause you crap in it," he said.

"No shit," I said.

I'd been learning some cuss words like my brother, but I wasn't near as good at cussin as he was, but I was making good progress. I learned much later on that the real reason that it was called a crapper, was because the name of the man who held the patent on the contraption was named Crapper.

"You piss in it, too," Willy also said to me. "So, go and get to peeing, and don't tell Pappy I called it a crapper."

I had actually seen one once before at the courthouse in Oxford before that day, but I didn't know what it was called, and had never used one. They still had outdoor toilets behind the cotton gin in Oxford, not far off the square. That's where I went when I had to go if we were in town for whatever reason, which was not but once or twice a year.

I peed in the commode, and my brother reached over and pushed the handle that flushed the tank before I was quite through. It made an awful sound, and I jumped a foot in the air, before watching the yellowed water disappear.

"Dang! What a racket! Where do you reckon all that pee and crap goes when it goes down that hole?" I asked.

"I don't know, but I'd bet there's a big pile of it somewhere," he laughed.

I was still looking back at the commode when my brother told me to wash my hands in the sink.

"Why? I didn't pee on my hands."

"Just do it," he said.

"You shouldn't of scared me like that," I said. "You made me pee all over the floor."

We both left the toilet laughing, and when we rounded the corner of the station, Pappy looked our way and grinned. Momma, still sitting inside the truck, smiled, too. Pappy always seemed to know what we were up to, and he always had ways to teach us stuff, without our knowing that we were learning something useful. I always liked to learn things by accident, rather than on purpose. I don't know why that is though. I had a feeling that we were going to have to learn things in a hurry when we got to Tupelo.

We pulled out of the service station just before noon, and got back on the road to Tupelo. Pappy never drove the old truck over twenty-five miles per hour, so it took a while to get anywhere. Pappy insisted that twenty-five was fast enough, and that the old truck might just fly apart if we went any faster. I contemplated on what a truck would look like flying apart, but couldn't imagine such a thing.

We had just passed through Pontotoc when Pappy saw a grove of big oak trees off to the left, and said that it looked like a good place to have lunch. He pulled the truck off the road, and parked beneath the shade of the oak trees. We climbed out of the truck, and Momma spread a bed sheet on the ground, as Willy and I began unpacking the lunch that she had fixed for us. Pappy reached under the seat and pulled out a sack of cold drinks he had bought at the gas station. He had bought Willy and me each a Sun Spot orange drink, and him and Momma a Coke. It was the first time I had ever had a Sun Spot, and it was the best thing I had ever tasted.

After we had eaten lunch, we loaded back into the truck, and turned back onto the highway toward Tupelo. For a while, we sat in silent reverie, as the roar of the old truck caused my eyelids to become heavy. I fought off the tired feeling, as a question tugged at the back of my mind.

"Why can't colored people use the toilet back there at that gas station?" I asked.

Pappy never took his eyes of the road, but he pooched his lips forward, and I could tell he was thinking mighty hard. Momma turned her head toward Pappy, and raised an eyebrow, her lips pressed together tightly, like she was holding back a grin or something. I expected her to speak, but she never did.

Pappy was a smart man. He knew a lot of things you wouldn't expect him to know, for he didn't have much schooling. He had dropped out of school when he was seventeen, got married to Momma, and joined the navy. He had intended to make the navy a career, and was preparing to have Momma come to Hawaii with us boys, when the war broke out. When he finally answered it was almost like he was ashamed to tell me.

"That's a mighty hard question, son, but it's a question that you need to know the answer to," he told me. "I'll try to tell you the best I can."

Pappy went on to explain to me that colored people were once slaves, like our ancestors were back in Biblical times, and they were often treated no better than animals. A lot of people didn't like slavery, but some people did. The ones that did lived mostly in the south, like we do. Those people used slaves to work the cotton fields, which was big business in the south. One day, President Abraham Lincoln proclaimed that there would be no more slavery, and that caused a war between the north and south. I know you have heard part of this story in school, and you'll hear much more in years to come, I'm sure."

I nodded, and he continued.

"We called this war the Civil War, because it was a war within our own country. There weren't nothing civil about it though. It was an awful war. To make a mighty long story short, the south lost that war, and there was no more slavery, but it didn't change most people's minds about colored people. They were thought of as being less important than white people. The war was nearly a hundred years ago, but that bitterness still exists, and the colored people suffer because of it. But what is worse, is that the bitterness will likely continue for many years to come."

"I read a book once by Mr. Ernest Hemingway, and he quoted some other fellow, something to the effect that 'no man is an island', meaning that every man is a part of the human race, and that if one person is allowed to be made to feel small, then all humans are diminished because of it. When the colored man is mistreated, it hurts all human beings in a way. It makes us all look smaller when we allow it to happen."

I hadn't known much about colored people, and there were only two colored families around Big Flat. I was old enough to understand that colored people were mistreated, and that it wasn't right. My momma had always cautioned me never to mistreat anyone, colored or otherwise.

Pappy didn't say anymore on the subject, and I didn't ask any more questions. In the back of my mind, I felt like there was a lot more to the story than Pappy wanted to tell me right then. I wanted to ask who Mr. Hemingway was, but thought I'd best wait. My flabber was plumb gasted to learn that Pappy had actually read a book. I had never seen him read anything but The Farmer's Almanac. Now I was wondering if he had read other books that he hadn't mentioned. But I didn't ask any more questions. My head was already so full of stuff to think about that I just didn't want to hear anything else today.

5

Meeting Mr. Purnell

IT TOOK US THE better part of an hour to get to Tupelo, even though it was only about twenty miles away. We crossed over the Natchez Trace Highway, just out of town, and after a while we passed the city limit sign of the town. Pappy slowed the old truck to a crawl inside the city limits. We had to wait at the railroad crossing for a train to pass. This was the first time I had actually seen a train up close. I tried to count the cars, but lost track after a while, because it was a very long, fast train, and I was getting dizzy just watching it pass by. After we crossed the tracks, we drove down Main Street of Tupelo, through a wide canyon of stores and shops, until the street started a rather steep decline. Storekeepers had already started putting up Christmas decorations, and there were a lot of people on the streets shopping. It was a sight to see.

About halfway down the slope, Pappy pointed and said, "There's the place where I'll be working, there on the right side of the street. Wayne has certainly built himself quite an enterprise here."

The building he was referring to was a large, wood frame building, with a large sign across the front that read "Purnell Lumber Company and Building Supplies". Just past the building, Pappy turned off of Main Street, and onto a smaller street, which ran alongside the lumber yard. As we drove, I spotted a drug store, an ice house, a dry cleaners, and a small grocery store, all on Main Street, across from the lumber yard. We passed other buildings that were a part of the lumber yard, and Pappy drove on for a little ways further.

At the fence where the lumber company stopped sat a small frame house with a front porch that spanned the length of the house. Situated beneath some large oak trees, the house looked as if it had a fresh coat of white paint. Painted houses were something you didn't see much of in Big Flat. Beside the house was a garage, and a small storage building. That was where the road ended. Beyond the garage was a wire fence, and just beyond that was a meadow where cattle could graze, and an open field where the land sloped downward toward a forest of large oak and sycamore trees. It was a beautiful place; it was a farm inside the city.

"This is it," Pappy said, as he pulled the old truck into the front yard. There were two large, ladder-back rocking chairs on the front porch of the cottage, and a tall, slender man was sitting in one, with his hat resting on his knee. A redbone hound came out from under the porch to greet us, and gave a single howl, as if announcing we were there. Mr. Purnell yelled at him, and he went back under the porch.

"That man there is Wayne," Pappy said to Momma, before turning to address us. "To you boys, it's Mr. Purnell, got it?"

Willy and I nod, and Pappy drives on. As soon as we had pulled into the yard, Mr. Purnell was off the porch. He walked over to the old truck as Pappy turned off the engine. Mr. Purnell opened the door for Pappy with a huge grin on his face, tickled to see him.

"It's about time you were getting here," he said, extending his hand out to Pappy. "Been waiting for awhile. I've heard talk that you drive as slow as a wider woman's ox, so now I reckon that's probably the truth." His grin was infectious. He then bent over, and looked through the window of the truck. "And how are you doing, Allie? Still looking out after this old reprobate?"

Without giving Momma a chance to answer, Mr. Purnell said, "You all get out and have a look around. I know you're ready to stretch your legs. I brought you boys some cold drinks. I set them just inside the screen door there. I brought enough for your momma and pappy, too. Old Man Epps has already been here and gone. We unloaded everything inside. Had some of the men at the lumber yard come over and help, too. We may not have put everything just where you want it, but it's all inside the house. My wife, Bonnie, will be by directly to see you, Allie. She said she'd help get everything squared away."

Momma thanked Mr. Purnell, and then disappeared inside the house, a big smile on her face. Our Momma was a pretty woman. She was small, with long, auburn hair, and dark brown eyes, the same color as mine. When it came to beauty, she didn't finish second to anybody, especially when she smiled.

"I brought you an old Frigidaire that we had sittin' down at the store. It runs plenty good. I hope you don't mind me doing that. It makes ice real good, and it'll come in handy when the weather gets hot," Mr. Purnell said.

Pappy didn't comment, but I could tell he was grateful, even if he wouldn't say it. He knew that Momma had been wanting one for some time. I don't think I ever saw a man so happy to see my momma and pappy as Mr. Purnell was. He was a tall man like my pappy with fire red hair and a freckled face. He seemed to always be grinning even when he wasn't. When we had finished unloading the last of the boxes, Mr. Purnell motioned for Pappy to sit for a while on the porch with him. Momma brought out the cold drinks, and passed them around to us all, before going back into the house, where we could hear her moving things around.

The house had a Frigidaire, a gas cook stove, and an inside toilet. We had never had any of these things in Big Flat, and it was plain to see that my momma was a little intimidated by the new appliances. She came out on the porch and told Mr. Purnell that she didn't know how to use the range, that someone would have to show her how it worked. I could tell that she was embarrassed.

"When Bonnie gets here in a little while, she'll be glad to show you," he told her. "We've got one like it at our house. She'll show you about the Frigidaire, too."

"That your hound dog, Wayne?" Pappy asked, gesturing to the dog under the porch.

"Not mine," Mr. Purnell said. "I reckon he comes with the house. I call him Squat, cause he ain't worth a squat. I feed him sometimes, but he mostly seems to live off the rabbits and squirrels around here. Don't think he knows the difference though. If he gets to be a pest, we'll call the dog pound and have them come and get him. He ain't much more than a pup. Guess somebody just dropped him off, and he thinks this is his home now."

After Momma went back inside the house, Mr. Purnell got back to talking to Pappy. Boy, that man sure could talk. Pappy had said he thought Wayne was half rattlesnake, and half cottonmouth. A rattlemouth. That had made me laugh, but now I saw why he said it.

I hoped that Pappy wouldn't call the pound to get the dog, for Willy and I both really liked dogs. We had a big, black shepherd in Big Flat, but he had died of old age two years back, and we hadn't had a dog since, despite asking Pappy a few times. Squat was plenty friendly even if he didn't know the difference between a rabbit and a squirrel. I didn't hold that against him. Pappy liked dogs, too, and most any mutt would take to him right off of. Dogs always seem to be able to sense the quality of a man after just a few minutes. They either like you, or they don't, right off. They always liked Pappy though.

6

Bonnie Purnell

IT WAS NEARLY FOUR o'clock when Mrs. Bonnie Purnell finally made it to the house. She drove up in a brand new, black Ford Custom. Pappy said he liked the new Fords, but he couldn't tell which way they were headed when they were parked. Mr. Purnell had said that Bonnie didn't drive much, and that she'd had the car for six months, had only put eighty-five miles on it.

Mrs. Purnell was about the prettiest woman I'd ever seen, aside from Momma, and I think Willy thought she was plenty pretty, too. She was taller than my mother and had golden hair and blue eyes. She was thin but it didn't take anything away from her beauty. She was nice too, and my momma seemed to take to her like a hog to buttermilk. Mr. Purnell had introduced Miss Bonnie to Momma, and the two women went inside the house together shortly thereafter. From the porch, we could hear them talking and laughing as they began putting things in order in the house.

Mr. Purnell and my pappy sat on the front porch, smoked Camel cigarettes, and talked about life, while the women worked to straighten up the house. Willy and I sat on the edge of the porch, our legs dangling over the side, listening as they began to discuss business. Mr. Purnell told Pappy that business had been real good since the soldiers had started coming home from the war, because they had been building new houses. He told him how, just last year, he had hired a new yard manager by the name of Bill Pickett, who had let the inventory slowly decline, until Mr. Purnell discovered that things were just plain missing. He had fired the man a month ago, and he was hoping that my Pappy could get the yard back in order and set up a better way of keeping track of the lumber in stock. He said that he wanted Pappy to learn every aspect of the business, so that when he wasn't there, Pappy could be in charge.

"Woah now," said Pappy, "I'm no good with books and business matters. You best just let me stick to doing the heavy work."

"You'll get plenty of heavy work, but I'm gonna teach you about the other stuff, too," he told him. "It ain't nothing you're gonna have a problem with."

"Well, we'll see," said Pappy with a shrug.

Pappy and Mr. Purnell started talking about baseball, specifically the Cardinals, and spoke for an hour about every player on the team. Mr. Purnell and my pappy both knew every single player's name, and everything else about them it seemed. Then the subject changed to music.

"You still got that old, flat top Gibson, AC?" Mr. Purnell asked.

"Sure enough, but don't play much anymore. Can't afford the strings," Pappy laughed. "You still saw on that fiddle, I guess?"

"Oh, I still get it out every now and again," Mr. Purnell said. "Bonnie likes to sing, so I play it some for her so she can sing."

"I guess she's a fine singer then?" Pappy asked.

"Nope, she couldn't carry a tune in a wheelbarrow with sideboards, but I don't tell her that," Mr. Purnell laughed. "We used to have a bunch of stray dogs around our neighborhood until Bonnie started into singing on the back porch. Every dog in Tupelo has done run plumb off. They had to go and rent some dogs from Pontotoc so they wouldn't have to lay off the dog catcher." Pappy and Mr. Purnell had good laugh. It was sure good to see my Pappy laugh after the sad times he'd seen.

"I think I'm gonna like Tupelo," I thought to myself out loud.

After an hour or so, Momma and Miss Bonnie joined us back out onto the porch, and Miss Bonnie announced that she and Momma were going to the grocery store up the street, so that she could introduce Momma to the owners of the store, and also pick up a few things. Pappy took his ragged, old bill-fold from his overalls, and handed Momma a ten-dollar bill.

Miss Bonnie turned to Willy and me. "You boys come along too," she said. "We'll drive by the place where you'll be going to school. It's just three or four blocks, so you'll be able to walk easy enough."

We got into Miss Bonnie's black Ford Custom, and she drove us down to the grocery store. It was not a very big store, not much bigger than grandpa's old store in Big Flat, but it had more canned goods and produce. There were even fresh bananas, which was not something we could easily get in Big Flat. The owners had a whole stalk of them hanging from the ceiling, and it made me excited. I always loved bananas, I truly believed that I could have eaten the whole stalk. Momma saw me looking at the bananas, and with a smile on her face, she bought two pounds. After Miss Bonnie introduced us all to Mr. and Mrs. Johnson, the owners of the small store, we paid for our things, and left.

Miss Bonnie drove up by the schoolyard. It was impressive. Much nicer than our school back in Big Flat. The buildings looked new, and the grounds were freshly mowed, and very plush.

"The front door is yonder," Miss Bonnie said, pointing to a set of double glass doors on the side of the building. Willy and I just looked at each other. "You'll find the principal's office just inside those doors, and the principal's name is Mr. Thompson. He is a very nice man, but puts up with no nonsense. He don't tolerate any misbehaving of any kind. They say he's got a paddle, and is not timid about using it." Miss Bonnie kind of made a side glance at Momma and smiled, but I didn't see any humor in it myself.

Miss Bonnie drove us all around Tupelo, eagerly showing us where they lived, places they frequented, and where they went to church. They had a nice house on Grove Street, with big trees in the yard, and a white picket fence across the front. It was nice, but it was not much bigger than the one we would be living in. She then drove by the movie theater, and promised she would take my brother and me when we got settled into school. That made us excited.

When we got back to the house, Pappy and Mr. Purnell were still sitting on the porch, right where we had left them. Momma and Miss Bonnie went inside once more and began cooking supper. We had fried pork chops, and skillet potatoes, along with purple hull peas, and a side of cornbread. Mr. Purnell really bragged on Momma's cooking, much to her pleasure, and I think Miss Bonnie was a little embarrassed at how much he had eaten. Pappy smiled and winked at Momma, and she grinned proudly.

After supper Pappy and Mr. Purnell sat at the table and drank coffee for a long time, talking about uninteresting business things. Willy and I went out to the porch, and sat in the big rockers, just listening to the sounds of Tupelo. Squat came from under the porch to lay on his belly between us. As darkness fell, we could hear a freight train passing through, its horn breaking through the silence of a cloudless night. The wheels clattered the rails as it picked up speed; all new sounds to boys from Big Flat.

7

First Day of School

MONDAY MORNING CAME QUICKLY, and Momma said she was gonna walk with us to the school on our first day. I think she could tell that I was a little nervous about walking to school every day. Of course, we had walked to school in Big Flat, but we could see the school from our house. It wasn't very far at all. This was going to be different, but Momma assured us we would be just fine.

"I have your report cards and shot records that I have to take to Mr. Thompson," she said to us. "I want to introduce myself, and be sure he knows how to get in touch with us if he needs to."

I was sure hoping that Mr. Thompson wouldn't find a need, for Pappy was real unreasonable about us getting in trouble at school. That was a contradiction, for Pappy was usually pretty reasonable about just about everything else.

We walked down past the lumber yard, just as the men were starting their work for the day. We could see Pappy through the fence, talking to several men who were gathered around him. Squat was at his heels on his haunches. We couldn't hear what Pappy was saying, but we figured he was letting the other men get to know him a bit. We walked in front of the grocery store, just as Mr. Johnson was opening the doors. He came outside to greet us as we went by.

"Morning, Missus Calloway. You all headed to the school?" he asked.

"Yessir, Mr. Johnson, we are," Momma answered. "Though I don't expect they'll learn very much, this being their first day and all."

"Well, I hope you have a good day," he smiled and waved at us, as we walked on down the street toward the school.

I turned and looked back after a bit, and I could still see Mr. Johnson, wearing his crisp, white apron, watching us until we made the turn at Main Street. I liked Mr. Johnson, but I'd never seen a man wear an apron before. Usually only women wore aprons, like Momma. I figured folks in Big Flat would probably frown on that sort of thing, but it seemed perfectly natural for Mr. Johnson to wear one.

We crossed Main street to Broadway, and turned left at the movie theater. There were posters of coming attractions strewn across the front wall of the theater, and the marquis proclaimed "Coming Soon: Song of the South". I had heard that story before, and sure wanted to see the movie, but since I had never been to a real movie theater before, I didn't know what to expect. In the summer, they showed old movies at the school on Friday nights in Big Flat, and everybody in the whole community came. It was a big event, but it wasn't in any theatre.

Momma went straight to Mr. Thompson's office as soon as we walked through the double doors. Momma was always organized, and she was good at keeping up with things. She had all of our report cards from our time in school in Big Flat, along with our shot records, and some other things that she thought Mr. Thompson would require. Though there were a couple of those report cards that I had hoped she would have held onto.

Mr. Thompson's office was at the end of a wide entranceway, and from the hall, we could see Momma talking to Mr. Thompson through a large window, which gave him a full view of the hall. After they talked for a few minutes, Mr. Thompson came out to the hall with Momma, and told us he would show us around the school, and then take us to our classrooms. He was a very tall man, and Willy and I almost had to run to keep up with him. Later on, someone told me he had once played professional football. I believed it, since he sure was big enough. I didn't get much of what was being said as he showed us around, but I did manage to learn where we went to eat lunch, and where the bathrooms were. He finally took us to our home rooms. He took Willy first, since he was in a different building, and then I followed him to mine. He knocked on the door, and introduced me to the teacher, who seemed surprised to see him.

"This is Mr. Calloway," he said.

That was the first time in my life that I had ever been called anything other than Zack, except for sometimes when Momma was put out with me, and she would call me by my full name: Zachary Christopher Calloway. She usually had her hands on her hips when she did that, and that's how I knew she meant business. I sure did hope that the teacher wasn't going to be calling me "mister" all the time.

"He's coming to us from Big Flat; his Daddy will be working at the lumber yard for Mr. Purnell," Mr. Thompson told her.

The teacher reached out her hand to me, a smile on her face. "I'm Mrs. Shell. It's so nice to have you. What do you want me to call you?"

"Everybody else just calls me Zack. That's my name," I said to her.

"Then I'll call you Zack," she said simply.

I liked Mrs. Shell right off. She was about the prettiest teacher I had ever seen, and nice, too. She too was blond but wore her hair in a pony tail like a lot of teenage girls were doing. It seemed a natural fit for Mrs. Shell for she looked very young to be a teacher. At our old Big Flat school, the teachers weren't much to look at, not that we we were supposed to be looking. Mrs. Shell took me to the front of the room beside her desk to introduce me to the rest of the class.

"Attention, class," she said to the others, quieting them down. "We have a new student joining us today. This is Zack Calloway, and he comes to us from Big Flat."

Everybody in the room looked toward Mrs. Shell. Two hands shot up in the back of the classroom almost immediately. Mrs. Shell nodded toward the first raised hand, which belonged to a girl.

"We already got two Zacks in this here class already. Don't he have another name, or are we gonna have to name him ourselves?" the girl asked.

The class laughed, but I thought it was mighty poor humor, myself. Mrs. Shell did not seem to get upset. She just pointed toward an empty desk and told me to take a seat.

"Why don't you just let me work out the problem with names. Zack is a fine name, and it won't hurt to have three in the same class," she said.

"Where the heck is Big Flat?" asked the boy who had also raised his hand, even though Mrs. Shell hadn't called on him.

"Big Flat is over past Pontotoc," she said to him.

Big Flat was nowhere near Pontotoc, but I didn't say anything. I figured if they didn't already know where it was, they probably didn't give a tinker's damn anyhow. I knew my face was red, but it quickly faded as Mrs. Shell resumed the lesson she was teaching. Every now and then she would look at me, and give me a quick wink and a nod, which made me feel much better. By the time the class broke for recess, I had almost forgot that I was no longer in Big Flat.

When lunch time came, Mrs. Shell told me to follow her, so that she could show me to the cafeteria, just down the hall. I could smell the food before we even got there. Time had passed so fast that I had nearly forgotten about lunch, or about how hungry I felt. Pappy had given Will and me each a dime, so we could try buying our own food on our first day of school. The cafeteria was a huge place. You could have put the whole Big Flat school inside the room. Even though it was jam-packed with kids, it was not noisy at all. I figured out shortly why it was so quiet. Mr. Thompson was standing at the back of the feeding line, watching over the entire procedure. It was a good lunch, and there was plenty of it. I got in line with my tray, got my food, and sat down at at a large table with several other students, who didn't once acknowledged my presence when I sat my tray down. A lot of other kids in the room were watching me, however. Mrs. Shell came by my table, and began introducing me to the other students, and telling me their names in return. She then told me that I could go outside to the playground when I had finished eating, and that I was to come back to her classroom when the bell rang twice.

I quickly finished eating, and went outside, eager to see the playground. On the playground, three girls approached me cautiously while I was standing by the water fountain. The tallest of the three was also the boldest, and the prettiest. She came right up to me, told me her name, and then the names of the other two girls with her.

"My name is Annabelle Owens. Everybody calls me Annabelle. This is Penny Johnson. Actually, her name is Penelope, so you can see why we call her Penny. And this is Jessica White. We call her Jess," she said to me.

"I never heard of a girl called Jess before," I said without thinking.

"Well, you've heard of one now," Jess said curtly.

"I… uh… I didn't mean nothing by it," I said. "I just ain't never heard a girl called Jess before."

The other two girls smiled, but looked a bit embarrassed. All three of them were very pretty. Annabelle was slender, with flowing black hair that was nearly to her waist. They asked me my name, and I told them. Since I didn't know anybody on the playground,

I walked away from the girls, and went over to the concrete steps in front of the school to sit down. To my annoyance, the three girls followed me, and sat down on the step just below. *Bold as a barbed wire fence*, I thought to myself.

The girls talked non-stop for at least five minutes, when Annabelle stood up and said, "Look! There's that McCullough boy across the street yonder!"

I looked in the direction she was pointing. There were two boys over there though, one large and stout, and the other a mirror of the first, just shorter. Both wore short billed caps, turned backward, and ragged, plaid shirts, buttoned to the top. They were seriously mean looking eggs.

"Who is that?" I asked. "And why ain't they in school?"

"Just the meanest boy in Tupelo," the boldest girl said. "Maybe the meanest boy in Mississippi, I reckon. And his brother is just a notch tamer, but he's plenty bad, too. Both of 'em are wilder than peach orchard hogs. They probably won't even let him in school. They're probably scared he'd burn it down, or hatchet a teacher or something. He beats somebody up nearly every day, and robs the kids of their lunch money. You better stay clear of him if you don't want to get killed." She looked toward the boy, now with her two fists propped on her hips, looking like she had a good notion just to go after him herself and teach him a thing or two.

I wondered what a peach orchard hog was, but didn't ask, 'cause she acted like everybody ought to know. I decided right then and there that I aimed to be plenty friendly with this bold girl. Well, I sure didn't want to get killed, and I aimed to make every effort to stay clear of that McCullough boy. Unfortunately, he was leaning against a sign post on the street that we walked to school

8

Meeting Albert Davis

WHEN THE SCHOOL DAY was over, and class was dismissed, I walked down the hallway to the end of the building, and waited outside the big doors for my brother to come by so we could be on our way home. When we came out, I rattled on about what the bold girl had told me at lunchtime about the McCollough boy and his brother. My brother did not respond. His eyes were fixed on the baseball field at the very end of the school grounds. There were several boys out in the field shagging fly balls, while an older man hit the balls, yelling encouragement. They looked pretty ragged to me. Most of the boys couldn't catch worth a flip.

We watched for a few minutes from beside the bleachers, and I could tell that my brother was really wishing that he could be out there. I knew for certain that he could catch better than most of that rattail bunch. Soon, however, we had to be on our way. We crossed the street at the end of the playground, and took the sidewalk that ran beside Robins Street, in front of Mr. Johnson's grocery store and City Cleaners laundromat. I saw no sign of the McCullough boys, and I was glad for that. I sure wasn't looking forward to meeting them in person. They looked like mighty bad customers to me.

We crossed over Main, and turned down toward the lumber yard. We paused briefly in front of a Christmas display in the window of the City Jewelry Store, where they had a display of wooden horses pulling a wagon. The wheels of the wagon turned, and the horses moved as if they were walking while the whole thing revolved. It was fascinating to watch, but we had to get home, because we knew our momma would come looking for us if we tarried too long. Keeping Momma waiting wasn't something you wanted to do very often. If Momma was unhappy with us, Pappy was likely to be downright unreasonable.

When we reached the lumber yard, Pappy was standing beside an old pickup truck by the entrance gate, and was talking to an old man in the driver's seat. Pappy had on leather work gloves and his usual fedora hat. When he saw us coming a big grin crossed his face. He smelled of pine lumber. The old man climbed into the old truck, but Pappy stopped him before he could drive off.

"Wait a minute, Mr. Davis, I'd like you to meet my boys," Pappy said to the man.

The old man shut off his motor, climbed down out of the truck, and put his hand out to shake my hand. His fingers were bent and knotty. He seemed old and frail, with a leathery, tan face, with deep wrinkles running all over, but his grip was firm. His hair was solid white, and he had plenty of it. His eyes were clear, and very, very blue. He was not any taller than my brother, Willy. His back was bent slightly, and he turned his whole body when he turned his head, as if it was painful for him.

"Howdy, boys. I'm Albert Davis. I live a few miles out of town," he told us, as he shook each one of our hands. "I've been talking to your Pappy, and I'd like it if you boys would stop by my place sometime. Plenty of hunting and fishing on my old farm. I'd be mighty glad to have you come out if you want to. Got some catfish in my pond as long as your leg. Some snakes in there, too, but they friendly and don't bother nothing." We shook his hand and thanked him for the invitation.

The whole time, I was thinking, "*I ain't never seen a friendly snake. I ain't never even heard of a friendly snake. I didn't want nothing to do with a snake, friendly or otherwise. If I went fishing out there, I aimed to wear boots up to my armpits.*" Squat came bounding when he heard our voices, and lay down on his belly right beside Pappy.

Pappy said he would just lay in the shade and watched the goings on till Pappy left for the house. Sometimes, Momma would call for him to come to the house if she had a biscuit left over. He would strike out in a run for one of Momma's biscuits. So would I.

Mr. Davis smiled at us. "I don't hunt much anymore, for my bones ache too much, but I still like to catch them catfish," he said. "Plenty of fishing gear out there if you fellas ever want to come." He shook Pappy's hand. "Been a pleasure to meet your boys, AC I know you must be real proud of them."

"Well, sometimes," Pappy smiled, giving us a wink. "Been a few times, though, that we've thought about putting them out for adoption."

"Well if you decide to, just let me know. I'll spread the word." Mr. Davis laughed.

"You don't want them either, huh?"

"Mite too old to be raising younguns!" Mr. Davis and Pappy howled with laughter.

"I've got to be going if I aim to get this lumber unloaded before dark," he said, climbing back into the cab of the truck. The engine roared to life, and Mr. Davis drove out of the lumber yard. Willy and I waved, and we kept waving until he turned the corner at the end of the street. We didn't know it at the time but we would see a lot of Mr. Davis in the days to come.

"Well, how did it go today?" Pappy asked, turning to Willy and me. "Did you learning everything there is to know, or do you think you'll have to go back tomorrow?"

"I reckon we'll have to go back for another day or two, but I guess we ought to know it all by Christmas," I said.

We laughed, and Pappy pointed with his chin toward the house.

"You all get on home now, your momma's been out on the porch looking this way about fifteen times already. She's a worrier, you know." Pappy knew the same as us about the importance of not keeping Momma waiting. "If Momma ain't happy, ain't nobody at our house happy."

Willy and I made our way to the house, and Momma waved to us from the front porch when she saw us coming. It was good to get the first day of school behind us, but I couldn't get the vision of the McCullough boy with a hatchet out of my mind, and I was still wondering what the heck a peach orchard hog was. The day had already began turning into a cold night. It had been a very warm fall, but winter was coming, and the little house was cold when we finally crawled into our beds for the night.

9

The Mccullough Boys

THE HOUSE WAS JUST as cold when the sun came up the next morning, and we shivered as we rolled out of bed for the day.

"You boys better bundle up good today, because it's supposed to get very cold. Maybe even cold enough to snow," Pappy said to Willy and me. "I heard that on the radio last night. They've got snow in Memphis, and they expect we'll get some by this afternoon."

"I like snow!" I said excitedly.

Back in Big Flat, when it snowed, we would get out of school for the day, because the roads would become impassable. But in Tupelo, it was a different story, because all the streets and roads were paved. *Shoot!* We probably wouldn't even get out of school if it snowed up to the windows. By noon, the skies had cleared, the weather had warmed, and our hopes for snow were dashed. The sun was bright when we left the house, and it sure didn't look like it might snow. Momma had fixed us sandwiches to take to school, because today was soup day, and we didn't like the soup they made at school. There was too much green stuff in it. Momma never put green stuff in her soup.

We turned onto Robins Street, nearing the Wakefield's Store and Service Station that sat across the street from our school, and I had just asked my brother what a peach orchard hog was, when Naught McCullough burst out from a nearby hedge that ran beside the sidewalk, knocking my brother to the pavement. He sat on my brother's chest, and pinned his arms above his head. Naught's brother appeared shortly after, grabbed me from behind, and put me into a headlock, choking me. I tried to break free, but couldn't escape the hold he had on me.

"Don't you boys know that this is my street you're walking on? I'm Naught McCullough, and this here is my brother, Notch. This is our street, and I didn't give you no permission to walk on our street," Naught said through clenched teeth. "Now, pay a toll, or I'll bloody you nose. Pay up!"

I was struck numb with fear, feeling certain that we were sure to be murdered, and we'd never see Momma an Pappy again. *Such a thing would never have happened in Big Flat*, I thought.

My brother was able to grunt to them that we didn't have any toll money, or any other money either, and that all we had was a sandwich that momma had made us for lunch.

"Well we'll just take that then," Naught said, snatching the paper bag from my brother's coat pocket.

Naught motioned with his chin toward his brother and said, "Grab his bag, and then let him go, Notch."

Notch pulled the bag from my coat and released me, but kept his fists balled like he was fixing to whoop me. I backed away from him cautiously. Naught still had my brother pinned beneath his huge bulk on the ground.

"Tomorrow, you will bring me a toll of twenty cents for walking on my street. If you don't bring it your number will be up," Naught said to us. He released my brother's hands, but kept his fists balled as he got to his feet. He backed away toward the hedge, but gave us a final warning. "You better pay the toll, or I'll beat you both to a pulp."

The McCullough boys disappeared back into the high shrubs, leaving my brother lying on the sidewalk, and me shaking in pure shock. Annabelle Owens sure wasn't wrong about the McCulloughs. They were some seriously bad customers.

"I'm quittin' school," I said to Willy. "I ain't gonna get beat up every day, or killed on account of getting an education."

My brother didn't speak, but I could tell he was thinking mighty hard. I was convinced that today would end my search for truth and knowledge. I didn't want my number coming up; I was sure of that.

When my brother finally stood to his feet, I could see that several students had gathered across the street on the playground, and had watched the whole thing unfold. Not a sole had come to help. When we had brushed ourselves off, we started across the street, and the crowd of students broke up and walked back toward the schoolhouse. In the crowd, I could see the bold girl and her friends. *Just great*, I thought. She probably thought I was a coward, and so did everybody else at the whole school.

"Don't tell Momma and Pappy about this thing 'til I do some thinking on it," Willy said to me as we walked toward the school.

"I ain't gonna tell nobody, but the whole school saw it. Pappy is bound to find out," I said. "Besides that, we got to be thinking about another way to school, or we got to run away from home. That McCollough boy is dead serious about a toll, and the only way we can come up with twenty cents is to rob a store or something."

"We ain't robbing no store, and we aint running away from home, or finding another way to school either," my brother said flatly.

I didn't like that kind of talk.

That day was probably the longest day I ever spent at school. I would catch the other students looking at me every now and again, but nobody talked to me. The bold girl and her friends didn't even speak to me at lunch time. I sat on the steps, hungry as a bear, thanks to the McCullough boys taking my lunch. I had no money to eat in the cafeteria either. I tried to think of what I would do if it happened again, but I could think of nothing respectable to do. It felt hopeless.

When the lunch period was over Mrs. Shell asked if I would take the list of absent students to Mr. Thompson's office. I gladly took the list, and walked down the hallway, through the double doors, and down the steps toward the office. I was just turning the corner of the building, when I ran smack into Annabelle Owens, almost knocking her down onto the floor.

"I'm sorry," I said quickly. "It was my fault. I wasn't watching where I was going."

"It's okay," she said.

Annabelle was carrying a box of erasers, and she had a white smudge of chalk on her cheek. It was cute.

"I've been dusting erasers for the teacher," she said, holding up the box. "Sorry. I should of been watching."

"You've got a smudge on your face," I said to her.

I reached to brush it away without thinking, and she quickly caught my hand, nearly dropping the box of erasers. After a split second, she released it, and I thought I saw a hint of a smile, as she looked directly at me with the deepest, dark eyes I had ever seen. When I touched her face, a faint smile came across her lips, and she touched the back of my hand as I gently rubbed away the white chalk. When she touched me, I thought I would faint dead away, and quickly removed my hand.

She smiled full out at my embarrassment. "Thanks," she said, as she quickly walked away. I was about to keep walking, when I heard her voice again. "I'm sorry about not coming to help you this morning when them McCullough boys attacked you and your brother. The whole school ought to be ashamed," she said. "I wanted to go and help, but Penny and Jessie begged me not to. They said I would get in trouble if I left the school grounds. I should have gone anyway." Her face was filled with regret.

"No, you shouldn't have come," I reassured her. "It wasn't your fight, and you might have been hurt. My brother says it's something that we have to handle ourselves, although I don't know how we're going to do that."

"I'm sorry you've got yourself such a problem," she said. "I really wish I could do something to help."

"Maybe we can talk tomorrow at lunch, if you're not ashamed to be seen in my company, that is," I said.

Annabelle smiled, but didn't respond. She rounded the corner and disappeared. I couldn't hardly think of nothing else but Annabelle Owens the rest of the afternoon. If the McCullough boys weren't enough to worry about, now I had to worry about not making a fool of myself in front of the prettiest girl in Tupelo. My life definitely was never this complicated back in Big Flat.

10

Willy Meets The Coach

By the time school was let out, the weather had warmed up, and the sky was clear. It looked like there would definitely not be any snow for us tonight. I waited for my brother, as usual, on the big steps outside the building 'til he finally appeared. He was walking slower than usual, with his head down, staring at his feet. It appeared that he was deep in thought. I fell in beside him, and we walked in silence.

As we neared thc baseball field, I could see the boys warming up, as they threw a baseball around the infield. Willy headed toward the field, and I followed. The coach was sitting at the end of the bleachers when we approached, and when he saw us coming, he motioned for us to come to him. He was not a very big man, but he had a little extra weight around his middle, and his hair was mostly gray. He had deep set, blue eyes, and he spoke with a little rasp in his voice, as if he were a smoker, or maybe had a cold.

"I been seeing you boys pass by here every day to watch us practice," he said. He nodded toward my brother. "You ever play any ball?"

"Some," my brother shrugged, eyeing the coach critically.

"Well, I could sure use an extra player," the coach said.

"I play some, too," I quickly reported.

"Sorry," he said, "but I know you attend Milam, and only those in senior high are eligible to play on the team. However, I could use a batboy, and someone to help me keep up with our equipment, if you're interested."

"We're interested," my brother said quickly. "Just tell us when."

"You own a glove? Maybe a bat?" he asked. "If you don't, maybe we can scrounge one up from somewhere. We're mighty short of equipment."

"We got our own gloves and bats," my brother said to the coach.

"If you want to try out for the team, bring what equipment you have tomorrow and we'll see what you can do." The coach turned and walked toward home plate. He picked up a bat, and started hitting fly balls to the boys in the outfield, calling each one by name as he hit. Them players couldn't catch a cold in Alaska.

Baseball has a smell of its own, like nothing else in the world. It's leather, and dust, and sweat, and grass, and a thousand other aromas that stir the senses like no other sport. My brother was so excited, he could barely contain himself as we walked home. He was walking so fast that I could barely keep up.

"Slow down," I said. "You're walking too fast for me." He slowed down some, and I caught up. "I know that getting a chance to play ball is real important," I said, "but what are we gonna do about our other problem?"

"What other problem?" he asked.

"The problem of getting killed by those McCullough ruffians!"

"That's not a problem anymore," Willy said simply.

"It sure seems to me to be a mighty big problem. Death is serious, and mighty permanent. I been thinking we ought to sneak onto one of those boxcars, and catch that freight train out of town tonight. Be a hobo or something. That's better than getting our throats cut or killed," I said.

"Them boys ain't going to kill us. In fact, the coach just helped me think of a way to solve our problem."

"I ain't heard the coach say nothing about them McCullough boys. I don't even know if he knows them boys or not," I protested. "If you got a plan, I sure would like to be hearing about it, cause if it ain't a good one, I don't think I'm gonna sleep much tonight. I was thinking that if we ever needed a guardian angel, he better show himself pretty quick."

"I'll show you in the morning if them boys come to attack us," Willy said.

I sure didn't feel no comfort in knowing I might die tomorrow at the hands of the meanest boys in Mississippi before I even learned what a "peach orchard hog" was.

11

Annabell Means Business

ANNABELLE OWENS SAT ALONE on the steps leading up to the school. She had convinced her mother to drop her off early, as she went to work down at the bank. She scanned the sidewalk across from the school playground and the hedgerow beyond. She saw no movement yet. A majorette in the junior high marching band, Annabelle had brought with her a marching baton, which was the only weapon she could think to bring with her without arousing suspicion from her mother. She had told her mother that she need to come to school early so that she could use the encyclopedias in the library for a project she was working on in her class. She had made up her mind that, if the McCullough's should attack the Calloway boys today, she would go to their aid. She didn't know if anybody had ever been beat up by a girl using a marching baton before or not, but she was going to help them, and it didn't matter if she got in trouble or not.

She had been waiting nearly fifteen minutes when a bus pulled into the school loading area and stopped under the large canopy. Her friends, Penny and Jessie, bounded across the playground as soon as they saw her on the steps.

"What are you doing here so early?" Penny asked. "And what in Heaven's name are you doing with a marching baton?"

"I aim to use it on them McCollough boys if I have to," Annabelle shrugged. "I'm not gonna stand by and watch the Calloway boys get beat up without going to help."

The two girls looked at her with eyes wide as saucers. They were in total shock.

"You're *what*?" Jessie demanded.

"If the Calloway boys are attacked, I'm going to step up and help them fight those outlaw McCullough boys," Annabelle said again.

"Uh, no. You can't do that. We won't let you. You'll get hurt, and in trouble to boot, if you leave the school grounds," Penny said, putting her hands on her hips.

"Well, you can't stop me," Annabelle said defiantly. "I don't care if I do get in trouble or not, and that's all there is to it."

"You must really like that Calloway boy to act a fool like that," Jessie said. "That's it, ain't it? You like that boy. You want him to be your boyfriend, don't you?"

"Well, what if I do? Anyway, he don't know it yet cause I ain't told him, but if them McCullough boys don't kill him today, I aim to tell him that he's my boyfriend, and he better be paying attention, and not be looking at no other girls."

Penny and Jessie were stunned at the revelation. They said nothing more, but just looked at each other and grinned. They both knew that when Anna set heer mind to something she was sure going to follow through. The Calloway boy may as well get ready to have a girlfriend.

12

A Mountain to Climb

WHEN MOMMA CALLED US to breakfast the next morning, Pappy was already at the breakfast table, drinking his morning coffee. We sat down and waited, while Momma took some fresh biscuits from the oven.

"You boys having any trouble at school?" Pappy asked, as he moved the cup to his lips to take a sip of his coffee.

Willy and I looked quickly at each other, wide-eyed. I sure was happy when Willy answered, so I didn't have to.

"Some," Willy said simply.

"Anything I can do to help?" Pappy asked. "Problems just keep growing if you don't get 'em solved right off."

"We can handle it," Willy said.

Pappy said no more on the subject, but we knew that he knew a lot more than he was letting on. Momma made no comment, but looked toward Pappy, worry filling her eyes. There was no doubt that Momma knew as much as Pappy about our troubles.

"We will be a little later getting home today," Willy said, as he bit into a hot biscuit. "Coach wants me to try out for the baseball team. He says that practice is about an hour after school. Zack is gonna help the coach with the equipment and other stuff. If it's alright with you, Pappy. And Momma, of course."

"It's okay, as long as you keep up your grades," Pappy said. "If you start falling down in your books, then your baseball career is over. I hope you understand that. Both of you."

"I understand, Pappy," Willy said. "I won't let my grades fall."

"Pappy knows we had trouble," I said to Willy as we started down the street toward the school. "You told him we'd handle the problem, but you're gonna get us killed. Them McCullough boys are a pure tribulation, and dangerous to boot."

"Don't worry," Willy said. "I've got a plan. We've got to face the problem, and we aim to do it straight on. Just do what I tell you if they bother us again."

"I got me a plan, too," I said. "If I see 'em, I'm running for my life."

"No, you ain't running," Willy told me. "I won't have everybody at school thinking we are a couple of cowards."

I could see the logic in that, but it didn't ease my fears one bit. Willy had his baseball glove hanging from his belt, and was carrying his Louisville slugger bat across his shoulder as we neared the Johnson's store. Momma wouldn't let me take mine until I had gotten permission from the principal at school. I was okay with that, because I didn't want anything to slow me down from running, and I sure would hate to have them McCollough boys take it from me.

When we neared the hedgerow near the Johnson's store, Willy and I were both alert, keeping an eye out for any trouble. My heart was beating so hard, I wondered if you could see it beating through my shirt. We were nearly to the store when Naught McCullough stepped from the hedges, with his brother right beside him, just one step back. They stood blocking the sidewalk, and I felt sick seeing them looming just in front of us. Willy did not hesitate a bit as he walked toward Naught with as much confidence as anybody walking toward sure death could muster.

"Stop right there, schoolboy, and gimme your toll, or I'm gonna beat you and your brother there to a pulp," Naught said. "I told you this was my sidewalk, and you can't walk on it without paying a toll."

"We ain't paying a toll, and we'll go over you, or through you, if we have to," Willy said. "Now, move out of the way!"

My heart nearly jumped out of my chest when Willy confronted him. Those two boys looked like two mighty big mountains to climb. Willy didn't even blink. I knew he was serious. Naught took one step toward Willy, and Willy brought that Louisville slugger off his shoulder so quick I didn't have time to spit. He brought it up between Naught's legs with a whoop that made me hurt from the top of my head, down to my toenails. Naught bent over and grabbed himself between his legs. Willy withdrew the bat and with another quick swing, caught Naught right behind his ankle, sending him landing hard on his backside. He yelled in pure terror, while his brother turned and started to run away.

"Catch him, Zack!" Willy yelled.

Without thinking, I did just as he said. Notch was slow footed, and I easily caught up with him, and tackled him to the ground before he could even get off the sidewalk. I got his arms behind him, and held him in a double hammer-lock, when he started to cry.

"Please, don't hurt me," he begged.

"You be still, and you won't get hurt by me. My brother may bust open your hard head with that Louisville slugger bat if you try to get up though," I said to him.

Just a few feet away, Willy was standing over Naught, with the big end of the bat pressed hard against his chest. Naught was begging for mercy.

"Please, don't kill us! We had to do what we did," he begged. "I'm sorry, but we didn't mean to hurt you much."

"What do you mean you *had* to do it?" Willy asked him.

"Let me get my breath and I'll explain," Naught said. "Only, don't hit me in my credentials no more. You probably ruined me for the rest of my life."

"I'll let you up if you promise not to try anything. If you do, I'm just gonna hit you again," Willy said threateningly.

"I ain't gonna stand cause, I can't," Naught said. "Just help me to the curb 'til I get my senses back. I'll tell you why we was doing what we did."

After Naught had caught his breath some he began to sob. "My momma's real sick, and our pappy ran off three months ago, and we don't have no money to buy food, or money to buy any medicine for my momma. I think she might die if I don't get her to a doctor. I went to the doctor's office to try to get him to come and see her, but that snooty nurse said If I wanted a doctor, I'd have to come up with four dollars. I was trying to get four dollars, but I ain't never seen four dollars in my whole life. I don't know what to do."

"I don't know what to do either, but my pappy will," Will said. "We'll go and see him right now."

"I can't walk right now by myself," Naught said.

"We'll help you. My brother will get on one side of you, and I'll get on the other, and we'll help you along. It ain't far to where Pappy works."

We supported Naught, and every now and then his brother, Notch, would take my place at his side. Naught was big, and he was heavy, and it soon wore me down supporting his weight. Once, I looked back over my shoulder at the school yard, and saw Annabelle, Penny, and Jessie watching as we carried Naught down toward the lumber yard. We made the four blocks, and sat Naught down on the curb. Willy told him to just sit there.

"I ain't moving nowhere," Naught said, "unless I crawl."

Willy went through the gate to the lumber yard to find Pappy. Naught was not feeling all that well, and we were going to have some explaining to do to Pappy. I was relieved that we were still alive, but Pappy might change that after we told him what we had done to the McCullough boys. If a whipping was all we got out of this, we'd be lucky. Pappy probably already knew about our run in with the McCulloughs, and he wasn't against us defending ourselves, but he didn't want us to be troublemakers. Sometimes, you just couldn't hardly tell the difference, but Pappy tended to lean toward the side of boys being troublemakers, and that could mean trouble for us.

13

Louisville Sluggers

ANNABELLE OWENS WAS WATCHING the sidewalk across the street from the schoolhouse steps when she saw the Calloway boys come around the corner by the Johnson's store. She was about to raise her hand and wave to them, when she saw the McCullough boys step through a hedge by the sidewalk, blocking their path.

"There they are," she announced, as she jumped to her feet, marching baton in hand. She started toward the street, with Penny and Jessie right behind her, calling to her to stop. Annabelle got to the street, but before she had the chance to cross, she witnessed something incredible; At the hands of Willy Calloway, Naught McCullough went down like a brick, while his brother was tackled from behind by Zack. She slid to a stop, dropped the baton, and both hands went to her mouth. Penny and Jessie grabbed hold of her, and the all three of them stared in awe at the scene unfolding before thm.

Students had gathered along the sidewalk as the the act played out. Those Calloway boys had made quick work of the meanest boys in Tupelo. She stood there, still in shock, and watched as the four of them stopped fighting, and started talking. She couldn't hear what they were saying, but when Willy Calloway stooped down to help Naught up, with Zack on the other side, she wished she could. She did not understand what had just happened, or why the Calloways were helping the McCullough boy down the street, but she knew that she had just witnessed something big. She was filled with emotion, and feelings she had never felt before. It would take some time to figure it all out, and get herself together, but she knew that she had special feelings for that Calloway boy, and she aimed to make sure he knew it.

Pappy saw us coming from inside the lumber yard gate, and came out quickly, with Squat right on his heels.

"What's going on?" he asked us.

"He needs help," I said to him, pointing to Naught.

Pappy and went to Naught, and bent down beside him, resting his hands on his knees.

"Tell me what's the matter son," he said to him. "What can I do to help?"

Naught quickly explained to Pappy what he had told Willy and me. Thankfully, he didn't tell him about the bat incident, but Pappy was a wise man.

"Are you feeling alright, son?" he looked Naught up and down. "You don't look all that well."

"Just got a bad stomach ache, sir," Naught answered.

Pappy looked sternly at Willy and me, with a knowing look. "Willy, you go get your mother, and tell her to come down here in the old truck. Zack, you and these boys wait right here. I've got to go tell the boss man that I'm gonna be gone for a while." He swiftly took off toward the office, and Willy took off running toward the house. I sat there on the sidewalk with the McCulloch boys. I felt a bit awkward being there alone with them, but seeing as they were no longer our sworn enemies, I wasn't afraid. We sat in silence until Pappy returned to the gate, with Mr. Purnell at his side.

"Where do you live, son?" Mr. Purnell asked Naught. "We're going to see what we can do to help your momma. It ain't right what your daddy did, runnin' off like that. We'll help you out if we can."

"Over on Lee Street, sir. The house is number twenty-four, but it don't have no numbers on it. I'll show you the way," Notch answered.

Mr. Purnell told Pappy to gather us all up and go on over there, and that he'd get his truck and follow, in case he had to go get a doctor. He told Pappy not to worry about work. He said that he'd get Sam Oliver to cover the yard while they were gone, and that Bonnie would take care of the desk in the office. They would be just fine for a little while without them. After just a minute or two, we saw Momma and Willy rushing out of the house, they headed straight toward the lumber yard in the old truck. Momma was still wearing her apron, and she had brought an armful of clean towels. Pappy opened the driver's side door, and slid in beside Momma. Naught climbed into the cab with them, while Willy, Notch, and I all climbed into the back. Pappy started the old truck, and we drove away from the lumber yard, headed toward Lee Street, following Naught's direction.

14

Helping Mrs. Mccullough

BEFORE HE LEFT THE lumber yard, Mr. Purnell had called Dr. Little to see if he would be able to come by and see what he could do for Mrs. McCullough. Mr. Purnell knew Tupelo like the back of his hand, and even though he didn't have Naught McCullough to give him direction to Lee Street, he said he would met us there shortly.

We took a right onto a narrow street, where I noticed that there was no street sign, and then took a left onto Peeler Street. There was a row of rundown, unpainted, shotgun houses on the road, with a mess of broken down cars and trucks, as well as piles of trash, along the curbs and in the yards. Naught told Pappy to stop, and Pappy pulled the truck to the curb midway down the block.

The McCullough boys bailed out as soon as we stopped, and ran up the steps of a nearby house. They flung open the door, and ran inside without so much as looking behind them to see if we were following. Momma went in behind them, and Pappy told Willy and me to wait on the front porch until Mr. Purnell got there.

From outside, we could hear Momma talking to Mrs. McCullough in soft words, explaining that her sons were friends with her boys, and that we were there to help, and that we were sending for the doctor to see about her. When my momma told her that we were friends with her boys, Willy and I exchanged a look. I thought about Pappy telling me it took very little effort to make friends, but folks had to really work at making enemies. I reckoned that was surely true. Two hours ago, we thought the McCullough boys were regular outlaws, and maybe the meanest boys in Mississippi. Now, they seemed just like regular people that loved their own momma, and were just trying to get by. I didn't know if I'd ever really like them boys or not, but I knew I sure didn't hate them.

After a few minutes, Mr. Purnell pulled to a stop behind Pappy's truck. A small man with a black medicine bag got out of the car on the passenger side.

"Boys, this is Dr. Little," Mr. Purnell said to us. "He's here to see if he can help Mrs. McCullough."

Dr. Little matched his name. He was no taller than me, and even Willy looked down to him. He wore a black suit, and a white narrow brim, western-style hat. He had a bushy moustache, and thick eyebrows, both of which had gray hairs sticking out. Actually, they were more white than grey. He barely acknowledged that we were there as he ascended the steps, and joined the others inside the house. It felt like ages had passed before he finally came back outside to talk to Mr. Purnell and Pappy. He was carrying his coat across his arm, and he looked concerned.

"The lady is very sick indeed," he said. "There is no doubt that she has a bout of pneumonia in both lungs. I have instructed her to visit a hospital, but she says she won't go. I have given her a shot of penicillin, as well as some antibiotics to take orally. However, she is going to have to have someone with her to make certain she takes the medicine. I will stop by tomorrow and for the next few days and check on her. She will need another shot tomorrow. Hopefully, she will be feeling better, but she is going to need a lot of rest, nourishment, and time. The poor woman has been reduced to bones."

Mr. Purnell stroked his chin, taking in the information.

"One more thing, the doctor added, it appears that there is no electricity or running water. With these cold nights, she needs to stay warm."

Pappy told Dr. Little that we would see to it that someone would be with her to make sure she got her medicine and proper food, and Mr. Purnell said that he would send to have someone turn the utilities back on immediately.

"My wife has some connections at City Hall," he said. "She'll get it done."

Mr. Purnell left to take the doctor back to his office, leaving the rest of us behind at the McCullough house. Momma stayed inside with Mrs. McCullough and her boys, while Pappy stayed outside with us. I could tell he was feeling a bit awkward, and he didn't say much to us while we waited for Mr. Purnell to return. I wanted to ask him questions, but though it would be best if I didn't.

The air had started to chill by the time Mr. Purnell returned, with a Tupelo Water Works truck following behind him. The worker climbed down from his truck, and without speaking a word, he went straight away to the meter by the street and turned the water back on. He walked to the door and told Momma to check the faucets to see if they were working okay, and then he looked under the house, and walked all around it, checking for leaks. When he started for the truck, he said that Jimmy Foster would be there shortly to turn on the power, and Pappy nodded.

Momma came to the screen door to tell us that Mrs. McCullough was sleeping now, and that she needed clean water.

"AC, take these boys back to the house and feed them. There's some fresh bread in the oven, and a pot of vegetable soup on the stove that they can eat. Fill up a fruit jar and bring it back here for Mrs. McCullough and me. I'll stay here with her to make sure she is tended to," Momma said. "Bring the m on back here after they eat, and then you can take Willy and Zack to school. They don't need to be missing their lessons."

Pappy nodded, kissed her goodbye, and told the four of us boys to get back into the truck. We drove away from the McCullough house, and I couldn't help but feel sorry for Naught and Notch, and for their momma.

We ate in silence at the table back home. Naught and Notch shovelled spoonfuls of vegetable soup into their mouths as though they hadn't eaten in a week, and for all I knew, maybe they hadn't. After all of our stomachs had been filled, Pappy drove us back to the McCullough house, where Momma told him to take all four of us to the school.

"Talk to the principal, Mr. Thompson, and see what all these boys need to be enrolled in school," she told him. "These boys shouldn't be missing out on an education."

I was flabbergasted over the thought of the McCullough boys being in a school, and I figured the folks at school was not going to be one bit pleased about them boys being there either. I for sure knew that Annabelle Owens was gonna be dumbfounded, and her friends would be terrified at the thought. I wasn't concerned that Annabelle would be scared of the McCullough boys, for Annabelle wasn't afraid of anything. I knew that she would, however, question the sanity of the Principal if he let them boys in school.

Pappy drove us to the school, and walked with the four of us to Mr. Thompson's office. After explaining our absence to Mr. Thompson, his secretary signed us in, and walked us to our classes, so that she could explain your absence to our teachers. Pappy stayed with the McCullough boys in the principal's office to see if he could help get them squared away for school.

"I'll pick you boys up at the curb when your lessons are finished," he had told us as we exited the office with Mr. Thompson's secretary.

The day dragged on and on. I got a lot of weird looks from the other school kids, but no one asked what had happened that morning, not even Annabelle Owens, who I hadn't seen all day. When school let out, Pappy was waiting for us at the curb outside the school, just as he said he would be. Usually, Willy and I would walk to the field together, now that he was playing on the team, and I was helping out, but today, Pappy told Willy to tell the coach that I wouldn't be there today. I was going with Pappy instead.

I had not seen Annabelle all day, since we had not made it to school until after the lunch hour, and I figured she was going to be sideways with me for not seeing her during the day to let her know what was going on with the McCullough boys. Being sideways with Annabelle was not a small thing, but I would just have to deal with it tomorrow. My head was already too full of stuff, and it was all rattling around like loose marbles.

Pappy drove us to the McCullough house, where he had paperwork for Mrs. McCullough to fill out, and instructions for what she would need to do to get her boys properly registered in school. Mr. Thompson told Pappy that he was going to go ahead and let the boys in school for the time being, at least until their mother could come to the school. Since the boys had not been going to school this year, they both would be tested for grade level. The principal said he didn't think the boys would be too far behind in their studies, but couldn't be sure until they had seen the test results. He said the boys seemed plenty smart, but a little rough around the edges.

Saying them boys were a little rough around the edges, I thought, was like saying Wolfman was a little hairy. The principal would find out soon enough that the McCullough boys were rough plumb to the core, and then some.

The McCullough boys stayed the night at our house, and slept on a quilt pallet on the floor. I woke up sometime during the night from Naught's snoring. I first thought I had fallen asleep on the railroad tracks, and was about to be ran over by a train, but that wasn't it. Willy was awake, too, and we seriously considered taking our blankets and pillows out to the porch to get a good night's sleep, but the cold air kept us inside, and we eventually were able to get some sleep.

The next morning, Mrs. Purnell relieved Momma from her duties of staying with Mrs. McCullough, so Momma came home to fix us a good meal of fried ham, and skillet fried potatoes and onions for breakfast. Once more, the McCullough boys ate like a couple of starved bloodhounds. It was a sight to see. Pappy watched them with a grin, but never said a thing. Momma watched without a single facial expression, but I knew it pleased her to see the boys enjoy the food so much. She was good like that.

Momma had told us that Mrs. McCullough had already started feeling better, thanks to the medicine from Mr. Little, some rest, and several servings of Momma's vegetable soup and bread. She was already up and walking on her own, and she even told Momma and Mrs. Purnell that she could manage being on her own. Momma told her that she would check up on her, and to let her know if she needed any help around the house, or a nice, warm meal for her and her boys. Momma and Mrs. McCullough had become fast friends since that first day, and spoke often. Momma even said that Mrs. Purnell had left a ten-dollar bill on the kitchen cabinet after they had brought groceries to the house. She said that she hoped Mrs. McCollough would use it to buy clothes for the boys. She seemed like a good, honest woman, and said she worried that she would not be able to find work to support her family.

15

A Job for Mrs Mccullough

ON SUNDAY AFTERNOON, MR. and Mrs. Purnell stopped by our house after church, and sat and had lunch with us. Momma had fixed turnip greens, cornbread, and a big pot roast. Mr. Purnell ate like he hadn't had a meal in a month, and even though Mrs. Purnell seemed a bit embarrassed, I couldn't blame him. Momma was the best cook. After lunch, Pappy and Mr. Purnell went to the front porch to have a sit in the old rocking chairs, while Willy and I sat on the porch, with our legs dangling over the side, much like we had the first night we came to this house.

"I've been meaning to run something by you, Wayne," Pappy spoke up. "I've been giving it some thought lately."

"What's on your mind, AC?" Mr. Purnell asked.

"Well, it's about Mrs. McCullough," Pappy said, referring to Naught and Notch's momma, who we had recently been helping during a bout of hard times. "We've been helping her with groceries, and general needs for the last couple of weeks, but we can't keep that up for long. We got bills to pay, and food to buy, too. The woman needs a job, so that she can feed her family. I been thinking of asking you about hiring her to check on loads coming in and sales going out of the yard, just to make sure what's going in and out agrees with the invoices."

"I see," Mr. Purnell nodded. "It's not a bad idea."

"I think it would tighten up our operation quite a bit, might even save us enough to pay her wages," Pappy added. "She might also help deliver some small loads on the short-bed. I haven't mentioned it to her, of course. So, she may not be interested, but if you approve of the idea, I'll have Allie get in touch with her and have her come by."

"How much did you have in mind paying her?"

"I was thinking twenty dollars a week to start, and a raise to twenty-five if she works out," Pappy stroked his chin. "What do you think?"

"Well, I put you in charge of the yard, and since you've come along, you've cleaned the place up. It's running like a well oiled oiled machine. I trust your judgment, and it sounds like a good idea to me," Mr. Purnell said. "By the way, while we're on the topic of wages, I raised your salary to forty a week, starting tomorrow. I don't see how Mrs. McCullough can feed her family on twenty dollars a week, though, so let's make it twenty-seven fifty." Pappy started to protest, but Mr. Purnell held up his hand. "Don't you worry none, we can afford it just fine, and you both deserve it." Mr. Purnell slapped Pappy on the back.

"Well, thank you, Wayne," Pappy smiled. "That's mighty generous of you."

Mr. Purnell and Pappy rattled on for nearly an hour about the Cardinals, and every now and then, Pappy would make some comment on their lousy pitching and spotty hitting. Squat came out from beneath the porch, and plopped down on the grass, and Willy and I ran inside to get out our gloves to play some catch in the yard. We stayed outside, tossing the ball, listening to Pappy and Mr. Purnell rattle on, until the air turned cold, and the sun started to set.

The next day at school, Annabelle and her friends were waiting for me on the front steps of the school. Anna told me to come with them, and that she had something she wanted to show me. I walked with the trio past the cafeteria, past the steps to the principal's office, to the corner of an old classroom building that was no longer in use. There was a narrow passageway between the building and the main complex. The passage was about two hundred feet deep, and no more than fifteen feet wide, and led to an overgrowth of shrubbery and tall hedges. At the end there was a narrow slot between the hedges that Anna led me through, down to a small, open area, completely hidden from the rest of the school. Penny and Jessie waited at the corner of the passageway as lookouts, just in case a teacher came our way. When we were in the open area, Anna turned to me.

"You want to see my panties, Zack?" she asked me.

My face got hot immediately, and my heart thudded in my chest. "Well, I-I reckon so," I stuttered, not sure about what my answer should be. Was it a trick question? Was she testing me to see if I was a gentleman? Or was she actually offering to show me her private parts?

"Well, either you do, or you don't," she said casually. "Which is it?"

"I reckon I do want to," I said.

"My momma bought me five brand new pairs," she said. Without any hesitation, she gathered up the skirt she was wearing, and brought it up around her waist. I was so surprised, I couldn't eve speak. I had never seen that much of a girl before.

"Well, what do you think?" she asked me.

"Well, that's mighty pretty, blue underwear," I finally stammered. "I ain't ever seen a girl's underwear before."

"Do you want to touch them?" she asked.

"Sure, I do," I said. I reached out to feel them, but Anna caught my hand, and gently placed it on her hip.

"They're nylon," she said to me, "the latest thing!"

"They feel good, too," I whispered, barely able to speak.

With that, Anna lowered her skirt, and led me back through the hedges. I stopped her when we were in the passageway once again.

"Why did you show me your panties, Anna?" asked.

"Because I like, and I want you to like me, Zack. My mother says boys are always trying to see girls' private parts and such. I don't want you looking at other girls though."

"You didn't have to do that, Anna. I already like you better than any girl I've ever known. One day, when I finish college, I aim to marry you."

"You seem awful sure of yourself, don't you think? I just might not want to marry you, Mr. Zack Calloway!" Anna teased, wagging her finger at me.

"Well, I aim to work on it anyway," I said. "Pappy says a little P and D will nearly always get you what you want."

"What's 'P and D'?" she asked.

"Purpose and determination," I answered. "You're the purpose, and I've got plenty of determination."

I walked away from Anna and her friends, just as the bell rang for class. Anna had her hands on her hips, and I was thinking I had gotten a right smart of education already today. Learning from books was going to be mighty hard for the rest of the day. I was not sure what all of what had happened today meant. I may have only been fourteen, but the picture of Annabelle standing there in her blue blue underwear would not soon leave my thoughts; maybe never.

That night, over dinner, Pappy told us how Mrs. McCullough had come by the lumber yard that morning, and how excited she was about being offered the new job. She had been so excited that she had even hugged Pappy around his neck.

"Yes, and I suppose you didn't do much protesting either, did you?" Momma poked fun at him with a little grin. "She is an attractive woman, after all."

"Well, I didn't want to be impolite," Pappy said, his face turning red.

"Uh huh, I'll bet," Momma replied, giving him a love tap on the jaw. I smiled, wondering if I would ever find a love like theirs in my life. Maybe with Annabelle.

16

A Gift for Annabelle

It was just a week and half until Christmas break, and even though I had no money to speak of, I wanted to buy a gift for Annabelle, and give it to her before school was out for the holidays. I had walked past the City Jewelry Store on Main Street every day on my way to school, and admired the window displays, but had never been inside. One day, I made up my mind that I would stop and see what they had that Annabelle might like.

When school was let out, I ran over to the baseball field, only to find it closed, with a padlock on the gate. There was a note was on the gate that read: *No practice until after Christmas break.* Willy was playing pitch with another player outside the fence, so I went over to tell him I was going on to the house.

"Tell Pappy I'll be there in a while," I said to my brother. "I've got something to do."

"What you got to do?" he asked.

"Business," I said casually.

"What kind of business?" he pressed.

"I'll tell you later," I called over my shoulder as I walked away.

I walked hurriedly to the jewelry store, pausing briefly to look at the Stagecoach display in the window before entering. As soon as I walked in, a very nice lady asked if she could help me. I told her that there was a girl at school that I wanted to buy a gift for. I was thinking maybe a locket, or something similar, because my momma wore a locket, and she had a small picture of my brother and me in it from when we were little. She wears it all the time, and has always told Pappy how much she loves it. The lady told me she thought the locket idea was very sweet, and that she had a nice, gold locket for twenty dollars available. Hearing how much it cost, I nearly swallowed my tongue.

"I don't have that much money," I said, hanging my head. "I can't spend no more than seven or eight dollars."

"Well," she smiled, "we do have a 10-karat locket for just seven dollars, and it is very pretty. It would make a very nice gift for a young lady, and if properly cared for, it could last a lifetime."

I asked her if I could see it, and she pulled it out from beneath the counter. She opened the small, white gift box, and opened it slowly. It had a gold chain, and the locket was about the size of a quarter, but was heart shaped. It sure was pretty. She said she would engrave a name on it at no extra charge.

"I'll take it," I said, "that is, if you can keep it for me till next Wednesday."

"What do you want engraved on it?" she asked.

"I hadn't thought about that," I said, trying to think of something that would fit on such a small locket. "I reckon you should just write to 'To Anna, from Zack'. I only have four dollars and forty cents right now, which I can bring you tomorrow, but I've got a plan to raise the rest of it by next week."

The lady smiled at me, and I left the store, feeling happy, but unsure. I hadn't actually come up with a plan to raise the money yet. On the way home, I stopped by Mr. Johnson's store, and explained my situation. I asked him if he had any odd jobs that I could do to earn the rest of the money.

"Well," he said thoughtfully, "I do buy back Coca-Cola bottles, and some other drink bottles, too. I'll pay two cents a piece for all that you can gather up. Will that help?"

"Sure would," I said excitedly. "I'll start tomorrow!"

At two cents a bottle, I would need to bring one hundred and twenty-six bottles to have enough to pay for the locket for Annabelle. I knew it would be quite a chore, and I imagined that those McCullough boys had probably gathered up every bottle in Tupelo to help their momma out, but I knew there were a few at our house, I'd seen a few on the street past the lumber yard as well. I had to find some other ways to make some money. It was hard on my mind as I made my way home.

I stopped at the lumber yard to check in with Pappy. It was my good fortune that Mr. Davis was there with Pappy loading some 2x4's on his old truck. Mr. Davis recognized me right off, and started in asking me about school, and when I was coming out to his place to do some fishing. I told him I sure would like to come out there, because I did like to fish. I then asked Mr. Davis if he would happen to have any odd jobs that he needed done that I could do to earn a little money for Christmas.

Mr. Davis scratched his whiskers. "As a matter of fact, I've got a bunch of firewood that needs stacking. I'm guessing it would take you most of a Saturday to get the job done. Would you be interested? It's mostly split hardwood, and it is mighty heavy. The pieces are about two feet long."

"I'd be mighty interested," I said. "What do you reckon a job like that would pay?"

"I guess it would be worth about two dollars for a job done well."

"I'll take the job," I told him. "That is, if it's okay with Pappy and Momma. I've stacked plenty of wood before, and I can split it with an axe if I need to."

"No, the firewood won't need any splitting, but I've got a pile of pine stovewood that needs to be split, but I reckon I'm up to that job," he added.

Pappy said it would be okay, but that I would have to be sure it was okay with Momma. I could tell that Pappy wanted to ask me what I was gonna spend that much money on, but he didn't. I knew he would probably ask later.

"Albert, we'd love to have you over for supper tonight," Pappy said to Mr. Davis. "Allie has told me to ask you to eat with us the next time you came to town. Might not be much, but it'll be good, and it'll give you a chance to meet Allie, and for us to talk."

Mr. Davis agreed to come by for supper. It was near closing time at the lumber yard, and Momma surely had the table already set before Pappy even walked through the door. She was good like that. Mr. Davis told me he would give me a ride home, and I climbed into the back of his truck. I noticed that Mr. Davis was getting more feeble with each passing day. He had difficulty just getting in and out of his old truck. Pappy said he ought not to be driving, or loading lumber and such, but he didn't think he had any relatives to help him, and no neighbors close by. He said we would start dropping by to check on him on the weekends to see if he needed any help. It was plain as day that Pappy was worried about the old fellow. He really liked the man, and he knew it would not be long before he would not be able to care for himself.

I rode with Mr. Davis up to the house, and introduced him to Momma, who had walked out onto the porch to greet us, still wearing her apron. She smiled warmly, and told him to sit down at the kitchen table, so that he could have a cup of coffee while she was finishing up supper. Momma was full of questions, but Mr. Davis was plainly enjoying her chatter. She poured me a glass of sweet tea, and I sat with them, waiting for Pappy and Willy to come home.

"Mighty good coffee, Miss Allie," said Mr. Davis. "I hardly ever brew coffee in the afternoon. Sometimes, I'll have a cup left over in the pot from breakfast, and I'll heat it up. Some folks say it keeps them up at night, but I don't reckon it bothers me. I've never had much of a problem sleeping."

Mr. Davis mostly rattled on, and Momma nodded politely, occasionally indulging him in conversation. Momma had fixed chicken and dumplings for supper, with a pot of brown beans and ham, and some hot cornbread. Mr. Davis ate a good, hearty supper, and bragged on Momma's cooking so much that she fixed him a bowl of chicken and dumplings to take home with him. We learn a lot about Mr. Davis during his visit, for he sure loved to talk about his younger days, and his wife, Mattie, who had died of cancer three years back. He also told us all about his son Jacob.

We learned that he and his wife both had been orphans. They had met at an orphanage in Georgia, and had run away and got married when they were just sixteen. He had found a job cutting timber, and his wife found work in a shoe factory, until they had saved a few hundred dollars. They heard about land selling for seventy-five cents an acre in the Mississippi Hill country, so they bought a pair of mules, and a worn out wagon, and headed for Tupelo with their few possessions. They bought a full section of the land for three hundred dollars. They had lived in their old wagon until they could build themselves a small house. They bought an adjoining section during the Great Depression for one dollar per acre, and he said that they sold timber off the farm, and built the house where he was now living. Neither he nor his wife had any relatives that he knew of, and their son had been killed in a airplane accident when he was learning to fly. At the mention of his son's accident, Momma placed her hand over her chest, obviously upset over the thought.

Willy and I excused ourselves after supper, so that we could go to our room to do schoolwork, but we listened to the conversation with our door open. Mr. Davis and Pappy talked for an hour or so. Pappy told him about how he ended up in Tupelo, after three years of bad crops. He also told him that he was trying to save his money, so he could go back to farming someday.

When Mr. Davis had had his fill of good food, and good conversation, he left. Pappy and Momma diligently watched him climb into his old truck. The sun had set behind the giant Oak trees, casting long shadows across the yard, but it was not yet dark. We knew that by the time Albert made it to his home there would be no light. Momma said she hoped he would make it home without trouble. Pappy nodded in agreement.

17

Working for Albert Davis

On Saturday, Pappy drove me out to Mr. Davis's farm before he went to the lumber yard for work. We turned off the main highway, about four miles from town, crossed over a cattle gap, and down the dirt road lined with pine, sweetgum, and white oak trees. The trees were in full color, but the leaves were falling, and collecting along the road beside fences for about a quarter mile. It was early, and the sun was just beginning to break through the trees, but the old Mr. Davis was sitting on his porch steps with a cup of coffee in his hands. The mornings had started getting cold, and I could see the steam rising from his mug as we pulled into his yard. Pappy didn't get out of the truck, but rolled down the window and waved to Mr. Davis, yelling for him to keep me busy. He told me he would pick me up as soon as they closed the lumber yard, and told me to be sure I gave him a good day's work. Mr. Davis smiled and raised his coffee mug toward Pappy.

I climbed down from Pappy's old truck, and he handed me the sack lunch that Momma had made me. Inside the bag was egg sandwiches, and a few other things Momma had packed for me, and I was sure looking forward to lunch already. Pappy gave Mr. Davis and me one last wave, before driving off to the lumber yard. I walked up to Mr. Davis's porch, and he raised his mug to me.

"Here, why don't you let me have that," he said, motioning to my sack lunch. "I'll put in the Frigidaire 'til lunch." I handed him the sack, and he took it inside, returning within seconds. "Okay, let's get you started on the wood stacking."

There was a mountain of oak firewood just to the north end of his property, behind the old house. A little further to the north was a long, tin covered tractor shed. Under the shed, Mr. Davis had laid out four rows of 2x4s. At the ends of each row, Mr. Davis had planted a fencc post to hold the stacks of wood. There was also an ancient John Deere tractor under the shed, which sat beside a smaller stack of pine stove wood. The stove wood was a familiar sight to me, because we had a wood burning stove, and several fireplaces, at Grandpa's old place in Big Flat.

"Now, be sure to keep them straight, and don't let the ricks lean to one side or the other," Mr. Davis instructed me. "I don't need them tumbling over." With that, he left me to it, without another word.

I labored for two hours, making sure to keep the ricks straight and tight. I had stacked plenty of wood before, so it was a pretty easy job. After about two hours, Mr. Davis came to fetch me, and told me I should take a break and get a drink. I sure was ready for a break, but had not made much of a dent in that pile of wood, so I took a short break. Five minutes later, I was back to the pile of wood. I had finished stacking the first row of wood to the top of the fence posts, and I was proud of my work, but I had a long way to go to earn the two dollars, though I was getting worn out fast.

While I was stacking firewood, I could see Mr. Davis splitting the stove wood on a chopping block he had set up. He could only split a couple of pieces at a time before he would have to sit and rest. He was gasping for breath after just a little exertion. I finally told Mr. Davis that he should just sit and rest until I finished stacking the firewood, and that I would split the stove wood for him, and at no extra charge. He was too tired to protest, so he just nodded and sat there, with his back to the wall, and watched me work until it was time to eat lunch.

When we finally stopped for lunch, Mr. Davis retrieved my sack from the kitchen, and brought me a glass of iced tea out to the porch. Mr. Davis nibbled on a cold bacon and biscuit sandwich, and sipped gingerly from a fresh cup of coffee, while I ate my egg sandwiches and banana that Momma had packed. When I finished, I leaned back against the wall and stretched out. Mr. Davis went inside, and emerged holding a pair of tattered, leather work gloves.

"Your hands must be getting sore from the splinters in that wood," he held out the gloves to me. "Maybe these will help some."

"Thanks," I said. "They sure will."

I eagerly pulled the gloves onto my raw, splintered hands, and noticed immediately that they were much too large. However, I didn't care, for my hands were hurting, and I was thankful to have them. Mr. Davis said that I would have to get back to work soon, if I wanted to be finished before sundown, but told me that I would find a couple of fishing poles and a worm bed behind the old shed.

"Grab the poles and a can of worms, and we can walk over to the pond and catch us a couple of catfish," Mr. Davis sid. "We've got some time, and maybe you can catch your folks a mess for supper."

I excitedly ran to fetch the poles and worms, and we made off toward the fishing pond. The pond was just fifty yards or so behind the shed where I was stacking wood, but even so, Mr. Davis had to stop and catch his breath twice before we got there. When we walked up to the levy, he sat down on a five-gallon bucket, in the shade of a willow, and began baiting his hook. I made sure to kept a keen eye out for snakes, but saw none. There were a dozen or so white-faced cattle grazing at the other end of the pond, where the grass was green and lush.

"Are those your cows over there?" I asked Mr. Davis.

"Yes, I guess I've got about fifty head scattered over the farm," he answered, not looking up from his hook. "Don't need the trouble of seeing after them anymore, but I just like to watch them graze. It's kinda peaceful watching them, you know?"

I didn't really think that anything about cows was peaceful, but I didn't say anything more on it. We had two milk cows back in Big Flat, and they were just plain ornery most of the time. I smiled at the old man, and baited my hook after fingering a large redworm out of the can. We both dropped our lines in the water, and in seconds our corks disappeared in the black water. When we brought up the poles, we had caught two catfish, each nearly long as my arm.

"Dang!" I said. "I've never seen such a big catfish!"

It took me awhile to wrestle the big fish to the bank, but Mr. Davis handled his with ease, and never even rose from his bucket. He had a piece of sawgrass rope in his pocket, and we strung the two fish up on the cord. I was feeling very pleased with my catch, and was already getting ready to bait my hook again, when Mr. Davis stopped me.

"We've got more than enough for a good mess here," he said. "Besides, we need to get back to work."

He took the catfish behind the shed, where he had a long workbench that was attached to the shed. I had cleaned catfish before, but not the way Mr. Davis did it. Pappy had showed Willy and me how to skin a catfish when we were no more than seven or eight years old, and I reckoned that I had never thought of doing it any other way. Mr. Davis had a wide meat cleaver, which he used to sever the head from the catfish with a single, heavy blow, right behind the gills.

"The catfish feels nothing," he said as he brought the cleaver down. "The cleaver cuts all the nerves from the head, and the fish doesn't even flap if you do it right." He then used a sharp fillet knife to make cuts along each side of the spine, making two filets. He then used the knife to cut away the skin. He did it in no time at all. "Skinning a live catfish is a lot of work, and ain't very pleasant for the fish either. This way, it's fast and painless."

I guess I had never thought about a fish having feelings, but it did make sense to me. Just because they couldn't scream and holler didn't mean it wasn't painful for them. I suddenly felt a pang of guilt in my gut as I thought back on all the fish I had ever cleaned. Mr. Davis took the cleaned fish inside the house and I went back to stacking wood.

It was nearly four o'clock when I put the last stick of wood on the stack. The air was cool, but I had worked up such a sweat, that it didn't even bother me. Over the next half hour, I split stove wood, and stacked it on Mr. Davis's front porch, right by the door. Mr. Davis sat and watched from his chair while I worked. He had said he was feeling poorly, and I didn't want him to hurt himself, so I was more than happy to do it on my own.

"That'll do for today," he finally said. "You've done a fine job, son." He took two, one-dollar bills from his shirt pocket, and placed them in my hand. He then reached into his pants pocket, and took out a battered, old change purse, removed a silver dollar, and dropped that into my palm."That's a bonus for doing the stove wood."

"You sure don't need to do that," I said. "I'm plenty happy with the two dollars you paid me, sir."

"I'll tell you what," he said, "why don't you climb into the old truck, and I'll drive you home. Maybe your momma will have some of those chicken and dumplings leftover, and I can talk her into letting me take a bowl home with me."

"I bet she does," I said to him. "Even if she don't, she'll surely have something good, and you'd be welcome to eat with us."

Mr. Davis went inside the house, and came back out with the catfish, which was now rolled neatly in a newspaper. After placing the fish in the back, he climbed in behind the wheel of the old truck. He was breathing hard, and his face was pale as a ghost. He tried to get the key in the ignition but was having difficulty. I was about to ask him if he was alright, when he slumped forward, hitting the wheel. The key fell to the floorboard, and the horn blared as his weight hit it. I called his name, but he didn't answer. I was finally able to lean him back against the seat to get him off the horn, but his eyes were closed. I ran to the house to see if he had a telephone, but couldn't find one anywhere. The old man needed a doctor, and my heart raced, for I was suddenly afraid he was going to die. I ran back to the truck, climbed into the passenger side, and pulled him over from under the steering wheel. I positioned him as comfortably as I could, then climbed in behind the wheel, took the key that had dropped to the floor, and with shaking hands, I started the old truck. I had driven Pappy's old truck in the fields in Big Flat, but had never driven on a highway, or a road of any kind.

I figured I had to try to get the old man to the lumber yard, so that Pappy could take over, and hopefully get him to a doctor. I gave the old truck some gas, let the clutch out, and the old Chevy lurched forward, bucking and jerking like a wild goat. I made a big, wide circle in the front yard, and managed to get the truck onto the dirt road, and then out to the highway. When I got to the highway, I had a hard time controlling the truck, and

I hooked left and right. I was very thankful that there was no oncoming traffic.

I crossed back over the cattle gap, and finally managed to get the old truck under control. Mr. Davis had not moved, or made a sound, the entire time, and I felt sick to my stomach. I had the speed up to forty-five miles per hour by the time I reached the outskirts of Tupelo. The highway was also the main street of town, so I had no red lights to deal with before we got to the street that ran by the lumber yard. I barely slowed down to make the turnoff, and I slid the old truck to a stop at the gate to the lumber yard, with the horn blowing. I saw Pappy running toward the truck, a startled look on his face.

"What's wrong, son?" He asked, looking into the truck.

"It's Mr. Davis, Pappy. I think he may be dying," I managed to get out. "He needs to see a doctor."

Pappy's face dropped, and he ordered me out of the truck.

"Go and tell Mr. Purnell what happened. I'll take Albert to the hospital," he told me. He then yelled for Mrs. McCullough to take over the yard, and told me get home to Momma, and tell her that he might be late for supper.

Pappy turned the truck around, and drove away just as I grabbed the fish from the back of the truck. He drove away faster than I had ever seen him drive. I half way expected the old truck to just fly apart. I talked to Mr. Purnell, just as Pappy asked me to, and with a worried look, he told me to go home to my momma.

"It's a wonder you both ain't dead," Momma shook her head.

I had just told her about the fiasco, and I knew that she was calling my driving into question, but I was just too exhausted to care. I went to my room, laid down across the bed, must have fallen right asleep. Sometime later, well into the night, Pappy finally came home, and Momma woke me up to ask if I wanted some supper. Pappy was already seated at the table, and Momma had poured him a tall glass of iced tea. I sat down beside him, and Momma poured me a glass of milk. We sat in silence for a minute, thinking of all that had transpired that day. My stomach was still in knots.

"I got Mr. Davis to the hospital, and stayed with him until the doctor got him in and got him on some oxygen," Pappy finally spoke up. "He started to come around some, but apparently, he had a stroke. It looks like he's lost some use of his arm and leg on the left side, but the doctor doesn't know yet whether it's permanent or not."

The knot in my stomach started to hurt, as I thought about Mr. Davis, being unable to look after his cows, go fishing, or split his wood.

"They gave him some oxygen and medication, but it's just too soon to tell what kind of damage the stroke did to him," Pappy continued. "They said we can visit with him first thing tomorrow morning."

Pappy and Momma continued to talk about Mr. Davis, while I just stared down at my plate. They were worried about him not being able to care for himself, since he didn't really have anyone left in his life.

"What will become of him?" Momma asked, "If he can't see after himself, what will become of him?"

"I just don't know," Pappy told her, reaching out to take her hand.

I hadn't been able to eat much, but Momma told me to get ready for bed. Willy had gone to a basketball game, and would be in later, and as eager as I was to tell him about what had happened, I was also very tired. I wasn't all that big on praying, but before I slept that night, I asked God to make Mr. Davis well, and I thanked him for letting me get him to a doctor without getting us both killed. I figured that was one miracle that the Lord had already performed that day, so maybe he would pull off another one for Mr. Davis.

18

First Kiss

By the time Monday came, there were only a few days left before Christmas break. Annabelle met me on the playground, and walked with me to the school. We had about fifteen minutes before class, so I filled her in on most of what had been going on with the McCulloughs, the problems Mr. Davis was facing, and how I had driven him to the lumber yard, all the way from his farm. Annabelle stopped dead in her tracks when I told her about driving him, and I heard her gasp in surprise.

"Wait. You drove him? What were you doing all the way out there at the Davis farm in the first place?" she asked me, placing her hands on her hips.

"Just stacking wood for him," I said casually. "He and Pappy are friends, and he's old and needed help."

Annabelle tilted her head sideways and stared at me like she knew I wasn't telling her the whole story. She had that way about her, but she didn't pursue the issue any further, and I was glad for that. I was never much of a good liar, and I knew that if Annabelle caught me lying, she would be madder than a poked bear. I quickly changed the subject, and told her about Mrs. McCullough's illness, and about the McCullough boys.

"They gonna let them hoodlums in our school? That's a pure waste of time to send them two knuckleheads to school!" Annabelle said angrily.

"Yep, they'll probably start after Christmas," I told her. "But they're gonna let them in class tomorrow to visit, so they can start learning their way around."

"Those boys need to be in school down at Whitfield, with all them other crazy folks. Or maybe even in Parchman prison. They both are outlaws."

I merely sighed. I wanted to be careful about what I said regarding Anna's opinion of Naught and Notch, but I wanted her to know that she should get to know them before she was too critical of them.

"No, Annabelle, they ain't really all that bad," I said cautiously. "They were just trying to take care of their momma the only way they knew how. I hope you'll give them a chance at least. Imagine if it were your momma who was sick like that."

Annabelle didn't commit to that proposition, but I knew she was a girl that was thoughtful about everything. If Annabelle thought it was important to me, she would at least give it a try. I also knew that her friends would follow her lead. She looked at me and shrugged.

"As long as they don't burn down the school, then I guess I'll do my best to treat them kindly," she said finally. "So long as they don't go attacking you anymore."

I smiled. I was proud to be able to call such a kind person my friend. Annabelle sure was a special girl.

Over the next few days, Pappy and Momma visited Mr. Davis at the hospital every day after Pappy got finished with his work, and even took Willy and me with them on the days when we didn't have homework. Mr. Davis was always glad to see us, because we were his only visitors, which made me a little sad for the old man. Each time we visited, he fussed some about the nurses not letting him smoke his pipe. There was no rule against it, but they were afraid he wouldn't be able to hold the pipe with the limited use of his left hand, and might start a fire or something. Dr. Little said he was doing well otherwise. It would be more than two weeks later before the doctor told Pappy that Mr. Davis was ready to be discharged, but that he would need someone to look after him. He suggested the local institution where the other old folks went when they had no family to look after them.

"Absolutely not," Momma said when Pappy told her what Dr. Little had suggested. "We are not putting him in that place, and that's final."

"Now, Allie, it's not up to us," Pappy told her. "It'll be Albert's decision."

"Well, he can stay here until he gets better," she said. "I'll see to him."

"I'll talk to Albert about it tomorrow, but it will be his decision," Pappy repeated.

I knew that the conversation was far from over, for Momma was a stubborn woman, and had dug her heels in on this one. Pappy always told Willy and me that moving Momma after her mind was made up was like moving an oak stump from the ground with your bare hands. It wasn't gonna happen.

On Wednesday, as soon as school let out, I went back to the jewelry store to pick up Anna's gift. As promised, the woman had the heart engraved with "*To Anna, from Zack*" on the back of the heart. It was perfect. The nice woman who sold me the locket wrapped the gift box in pretty, Christmas wrapping paper, and tied it up with a bow. She then put a small tag on it, and wrote my name in fancy letters. When she handed it to me, I was as happy as a hound dog with a biscuit.

The next day, school was let out at noon to start the Christmas break. When the bell rang at noon, Anna was waiting for me with her friends at the bottom of the steps. When they saw me approaching, the other girls smiled and went on their way. I walked with Anna down to the pick-up stop, and asked her what she was doing over the holidays.

"We always go down to my grandparents, in Columbus for Christmas Eve and Christmas Day, but the rest of the time, my momma will be working, so I won't be doing much. Why don't you call me sometime, and maybe we can meet and go to the movies, or maybe go and get a milkshake."

"I'd like to do that," I said, "but we don't have a telephone at our house. I guess Mr. Purnell might let me use the phone at the lumber yard though."

"You could just come over here some Saturday afternoon if you wanted to," Anna said sweetly. "Momma would probably let us go for a walk. Or maybe we could sit on the porch and just talk."

"I'd sure like that," I said.

Anna gave me her telephone number, written on the back of her school picture. The picture was a year old, but I was happy to get it. Anna turned to go, and I stopped her.

"Wait," I grabbed her arm gently. "Before you go, I have something for you. A gift."

I took the tiny box from my jacket pocket and handed it to her.

"I can't take it," she said. "I didn't get you nothing."

"That's fine. I wasn't expecting anything. Anna—do you mind if I call you Anna?" I asked. She nodded. "Anna, I like you a lot, and I wanted to be the first boy to give you a special gift. I want you to take it."

Anna started opening the gift, a big grin on her face.

"No, I don't mind you calling me Anna," she said. "I like it when you call me that. You're the only one who does that."

"It's not much, but I do hope you like it," I said, watching her unwrap the box. "My momma has one, and she has a picture of Willy and me in it. She loves hers."

Annabelle took the heart-shaped locket from the box, her eyes wide as saucers.

"Oh, Zack, I love it!" she said. Before I had a chance to react, she threw her arms around my neck, and kissed me square on the lips. "Will you put it on me?"

Anna lifted her hair up, and with trembling hands, I clasped the locket around her neck. Her smile was so big, it put the sun to shame. Anna spun around happily, and it was then that I noticed Anna's momma standing just a few feet away. Judging by how she was standing, with her hands on her hips, and a frown on her face, she had been there to witness Anna kiss me. Pappy always said that it's never a good sign when a momma has her hands on her hips.

"I'll see you later, Zack!" Anna called over her shoulder, as she skipped to her momma's car, her new locket glistening in the sunshine.

I hoped that she wouldn't be in too much trouble with her momma, but I couldn't help but think that I'd probably let her momma whoop me with a log chain for another kiss from Annabelle

19

Christmas in Big Flat

IT WAS JUST THREE days before Christmas, and Pappy had already made plans to go to Big Flat to see grandpa for Christmas, but Mr. Davis was still recovering in the hospital, so on Saturday morning, we all went down to visit with him before we left for Big Flat. Momma brought him a box of goodies—baked oatmeal cookies, chocolate fudge candy, and a jar of pickled peaches. Pappy made the old man a walking cane out of a piece of white oak lumber that he had found down at the lumber yard. He had sanded and stained the stick until it shined just like the store-bought canes. It was a nice piece of work.

Willy and I had no money to spend on gifts, so we worked together to make Mr. Davis a handwritten card, wishing him a Merry Christmas. We even put a picture of Willy and me with our new baseball bats, which Momma had taken last Christmas. The old man was touched, and as hard as he tried not to show his emotions, I noticed a little wetness on his cheeks as he thanked us. Momma cried a bit, too, at our gesture, and that made me feel like we had done something really nice.

We stayed with Mr. Davis for more than an hour, until he had sampled all of the cakes and cookies, and told him all about our plans for Christmas. After a while, we said our goodbyes, Momma hugged the old man's neck, and we left the room, all of us feeling a little sad, and wishing he could just go with us. Pappy stopped to speak to Dr. Little in the hallway for a minute before we left, but never mentioned to us what they were talking about. Pappy would tell us, if and when, when he was ready.

We rolled into Big Flat a little after noon, and pulled into grandpa's drive, parking the truck beneath the big oak tree, just east of the old house. Grandpa came out the side door and down the steps to greet us, with aunt Zula right behind him. Aunt Zula was drying her hands on her apron as she came across the yard, and grandpa was grinning like a tomcat drinking buttermilk. They helped us unload our bags from the old truck, and Willy and I headed for the little room that we always called our own when we lived there. Aunt Zula had not changed it much since we had moved. We sat side-by-side on the bed for a while, recalling memories of things that had happened while we were living there, all that time ago. It felt like we had lost something in our lives that we could never get back.

I'd never seen anybody as happy as grandpa was to see Pappy and Momma again. I guess he was glad to see Willy and me, too, but it seemed kind of like grandpa had lost something very valuable and had suddenly found it again. It was the first time I had ever seen grandpa put his arms around Pappy. It was something I wouldn't soon forget. Pappy and grandpa went to the big back porch and sat in the rockers to visit. Grandpa filled his pipe with tobacco, struck a match off the side of the rocker, and soon had the pipe curling smoke circles into the crisp, afternoon air, giving off that sweet aroma that we had grown so accustomed to. We were home.

After catching up with grandpa for a bit on the porch, Willy told Pappy that we wanted to go down to the school to walk around for a little, and maybe stop by the old store.

"Go ahead," Pappy said with a nod. "Don't be gone too long though. Your aunt Zula will surely have supper ready before long."

Making our way toward the school, everything looked exactly the same as it did when we had left. That's when it hit me that we had only been away from Big Flat for just barely a month, even though it felt like so much longer. We spent an hour or so visiting the old stops that we had frequented many times in the past, including the school, which we knew so well. It felt good to be back in the familiar setting, but we knew it was only temporary. As the air began to grow colder, we headed back up the dirt road toward grandpa's house, eager to eat some of momma's and Aunt Zula's Christmas dinners. Of all the things I had been missing from Big Flat, big family dinners at grandpaw's house was one of the top.

Pappy and Momma spent the rest of Saturday, and most of Sunday, visiting with grandpa and aunt Zula, just enjoying each other's company. During our visit, neighbors from all around Big Flat stopped by to say hello whenever they saw Pappy's old truck sitting in the yard. Entertaining visitor after visitor, they would all gather on the back porch, and just laugh and talk for awhile, as though it were a big family reunion. Aunt Zula would make coffee, iced tea, and cookies, and she and Momma stayed busy serving up the refreshments. They were both grinning like schoolgirls the entire time.

It was nearly sunset on Sunday night when everyone had finally drifted away, leaving with hugs and handshakes, and promises to reunite again soon. After the crowd had cleared out, we had a big supper at the same old pine table that we had eaten at for most of our life. A faded picture of The Last Supper still hung on the wall behind Grandpa's chair.

On Christmas Day, we had a huge lunch, and exchanged gifts as soon as we had all finished eating our fill. Grandpa gave Willy and me each two silver dollars, and Pappy and Momma received a smoked ham, and a side of bacon. Pappy and Momma had given grandpa a new pipe, and a case of Velvet smoking tobacco.He was certainly pleased with his gift. Momma had made aunt Zula a handmade, fancy apron, which she was pretty pleased to receive as well. They carried on about the gifts, but the real happiness came from just being together for Christmas once again.

It was a little after two o'clock when we started getting ready to leave Big Flat. Aunt Zula was crying when Momma hugged her goodbye, and grandpa looked like he might do the same when he and Pappy shook hands. They all made sure not to let the farewells drag on, but assured each other that we would be visiting again soon. Before long, we were back on the road, leaving Big Flat behind us once more.

Tupelo's Main Street had been decorated with strings of lights and garland, and nearly every store in town was decked out with the same. Seasons greetings shone in nearly every store window. A few stores were open, but most had been closed for the holiday, and the streets were mostly empty. We pulled into the yard, unloaded our gifts, and Pappy kissed Momma, telling her that he was going to the hospital to check in on Mr. Davis. He climbed back in the old truck, and drove off.

By the time Pappy returned from the hospital, Momma had made hot chocolate and cookies for all of us, which had become a bit of a Christmas tradition in our house. Pappy had chopped down a tree from the Davis farm, and set it up in the living room before Christmas, for us to decorate. It was native cedar tree, and made the whole house smell like Christmas. Pappy and Momma had bought Willy and me both new Barlow pocket knives, and some calf-high, leather lace up boots. Pappy got a new pair, too. Momma got a dresser set from Pappy, and a bottle of sweet perfume, and I felt bad that I couldn't afford to get her something on my own.

Finally, there was just one gift left beneath the tree. A large, wrapped box sat near the back of the tree, against the wall, with a gift tag from Mr. and Mrs. Purnell, addressed to us all. Pappy told Momma that she could be the one to open the gift, since she had decorated the tree, which didn't make a whole lot of sense to me, but she was more than happy to open it. She took her own good time, too, making sure she saved every piece of the wrapping paper and ribbons. Willy and I probably would just have shredded the thing.

With a faint look of confusion on her face, Momma finished unwrapping the gift. Inside the large box was a brand new, twelve inch Philco television set. There was a card attached from the Purnells, which read, "*Thanks for all the hard work you've done this year, and for you kind and loving friendship. We love you all.*" You could have knocked the lot of us over with a flick of a finger. Willy and I couldn't wait to get it going, but we'd have to wait to get an antenna, and that couldn't be until tomorrow. So we just stared at it.

"What is that thing?" Momma asked.

"It's a television, Momma," Willy said in disbelief.

"Huh. I've never seen one before," she said, eyeing the television. "I've heard about them though. I don't think anybody in Big Flat owned a television. Do you know, AC?"

Pappy simply shrugged.

We spent the whole next day putting up an antenna, and stringing up all the various wires, so that we could use our new television. It was about dark by the time we finally got it fully set up. We were only able to get just one channel, so we sat and watched whatever was on. Several times, Pappy muttered something about not having time to watch such a fool thing, but he sure changed his mind when they showed a baseball game.

20

Anna Opens Up to Her Mother

ANNABELLE OWENS SAT AT the kitchen table, nursing a small glass of milk, and a few wafer cookies, which sat on a napkin before her. Her mother faced her, with her back against the kitchen stove, and her arms crossed across her chest. She was plainly upset with Annabelle.

"What on earth were you thinking, young lady, kissing that boy on the lips right in front of the whole school? You should be ashamed of yourself," she scolded.

"Well, I'm not ashamed of kissing him," Annabelle said calmly. "I love him!

"You love him? You're fourteen! How can you be in love with that boy?"

"What? Are you saying that a fourteen-year-old can't be in love with someone?" Annabelle demanded.

"Anyway, I'll be fifteen in a month. You've always told me that the more you love, the more love you have to give. I know that you can't give any one person all your love, but I know that Zack has my heart as completely as I can give it. The truth is, he has hardly touched me, but I long for him to. Even just to touch my hand. I don't want you to be angry with me. Will you just let me tell you about him?"

Tears rolled down Annabelle's cheeks, and fell onto the napkin in front of her. Her mother then realized that, even though she was upset with her only daughter, she needed to try to listen to what she had to say. So, she sat down at the table beside her, and put her hand on Annabelle's arm comfortingly.

"Yes, Annabelle, I'll listen. Tell me about this boy."

Annabelle related to her mother about how the Calloway boys had been attacked by the McCullough ruffians on their first day of school, and how they had been terrorizing and robbing school kids of their lunches, and threatening to beat them up if they didn't pay tribute. She told her about how, on just their second day of school, Zack and Willy were ready for them, and that they turned the tables, and thrashed those two outlaws with no problem at all. Annabelle told her about how Zack had told her that the Calloway boys had only been doing what they thought was the only way to try to get food for their momma, who was sick, and they had no money for anything.

"They got in a big scuffle, and the next thing we knew, there was a bunch of us watching from across the street. I was ashamed that none of us had gone to their aid the day before, but Zack told me later that they carried him down to the lumber yard where his father worked, and got his father and his mother to go see about their momma. She was in a bad way with double pneumonia. They were able to get a doctor to come and give her medication. Zack's mother stayed with her until she recovered. They fed the McCullough boys, and brought food for Mrs. McCullough—even paid to have the water and electricity turned on," Annabelle told her mother. She sat in silence, listening closely as Annabelle continued with her story.

"One day, I had been sent to dust erasers for Mrs. Collins, our teacher, and when I had finished, I nearly bumped right into Zack. He brushed some chalk off my cheek. I went back to the classroom, but I couldn't keep myself from thinking about him, momma. I think he felt something, too, because his hand was shaking when he touched me."

To Mrs. Owen's shock and horror, Annabelle went on to tell her mother how she had raised her dress, and showed Zack Calloway her new panties behind the school, and how he had been a gentleman about it, telling her that she didn't have to do that. Annabelle blushed, admitting that she knew it was foolish. She said that she had felt like a ten-yesr-old after it was over.

She even showed her mother the locket from Zack. Her mother sat beside her, and the only thing she could do was bury her head in her arms, unable to think of anything to say. She recalled being a young girl once herself, and could understand some of her daughter's feelings, but so much worry hung heavily on her mind.

Annabelle went on to tell her mother about Albert Davis, and how Zack had saved his life by driving him to Tupelo from his farm, and how he stepped in to defend their teacher when her estranged, ex-husband tried to attack her in the classroom.

"He's a hero, momma," Annabelle smiled. "I just feel like God made Zack just for me. Do you understand now?"

"I think I understand, Annabelle," Mrs. Owens sighed, "I just don't want you to do anything foolish."

"I don't mean to do anything foolish, but I can't help feeling foolish every time he looks at me," Annabelle gushed.

Her mother laughed, stood from her chair, and pulled her daughter into a tight embrace. "You're going to be just fine, baby. That much I know. Thank you for telling me about this Zack Calloway boy. I aim to make a point of getting to know that whole family myself, and maybe we can all sit and have supper together one night. You need to bring that boy by and let me meet him though. I need to get to know the one that's stolen my daughter's heart."

Annabelle smiled, feeling a massive weight lift from her shoulders. "I will, and I just know you'll love him, too."

21

A New House Guest

SCHOOL WAS OUT FOR an entire week after Christmas, and Momma let us sleep later in the day than she usually would when school was in session. However, on the day after Christmas, we were awakened a little after seven o'clock by loud pounding coming from the back porch. Hearts pounding, Willy and I were out of bed, and standing in the middle of the kitchen, within seconds.

"What's going on, Momma?" Willy asked, rubbing his eyes sleepily. "What are they doing to the porch?"

"Your father is having it enclosed and sealed, making a place for Albert to stay while he's recovering from his stroke. He said that the men at the lumber yard were not very busy, what with the holidays and all, and they should have the work done in a couple of days. This way,

I can help Albert with his medicine, and see to it that he gets plenty of proper food to eat. You, Willy, and your father will go out in the evenings and see to his livestock until he's able to get around again."

Willy and I exchanged looks. Momma had won after all, just as I expected she would, for when it came to pleasing Momma, Pappy was a complete pushover. I was glad that Mr. Davis was going to be staying with us for a while. He was filled with stories about the old days, and he loved joking with Willy and me. It was also plain as day that he was crazy about our momma and her cooking, just like everyone else.

The men from the lumber yard had the little room enclosed, and a brand new rug put down on the floor, by noon the next day. Pappy and Momma went out to Mr. Davis's house on the farm to up the small cot that Albert had been sleeping on, as well as a small table that he could use as a night stand. Momma set him out a wash basin, and a water pitcher, and made up his bed for him. They had the little room fully prepared when Pappy picked Mr. Davis up from the hospital. Momma, Willy and I stood on the front porch and watched as Pappy drove into the yard, and helped Mr. Davis out of the truck, and up the front steps.

Momma hugged the old man at the top of the steps, and then led him inside to the little room. I couldn't help but notice how he looked more frail and sickly than usual. Momma had placed one of the ladder back rockers from the front porch beside his bed, and had brought his Bible and his pipe tobacco from the farm house, and had them sitting on the nightstand. Mr. Davis smiled, even though the act appeared to pain him. I could tell that the old man was mighty touched by the care and attention that our family was taking to make him feel at home.

Willy and I went to the lumber yard the next morning with Pappy. Squat followed on our heels, as though he was one of the family, which he practically was at that point. He was dumb as a tree stump, but he liked us all, and his company always made me smile. We helped Pappy straighten up some lumber bins, and then sat on a bundle of two-by-fours and enjoyed Nugrape soda and some peanuts. A little after lunchtime, Dr. Little stopped by the lumber yard and talked to Pappy about Mr. Davis, and even though we knew we shouldn't, Willy and I listened to the conversation. The doctor spoke in a somber tone, and told Pappy that the old man had surely had a bad stroke the day we had brought him to the hospital. Not only had the stroke been severe, but Dr. Little estimated that it was not his first. He mentioned that Mr. Davis may start having smaller strokes more frequently in the coming days, and that he needed to be watched very carefully.

"Unfortunately, there is very little than can be done for him," Dr. Little said. "I have given him some medications to take, but with the extensive damage that these strokes have done to his body, I doubt that they will help much. At this point, his heart is just too weak. I recommend that he gets his affairs in order."

"How do I tell a man that he is going to die?" Pappy asked him, running his hand through his hair.

"I've already spoken to Albert," Dr. Little nodded. "He is aware of his condition, and what is to come. I've advised him to speak to an attorney, and I do believe he's already done that. Just be there for him, and watch him closely. That's all that can be done."

Pappy shook his head, clearly distressed by the news. I wondered how Momma would take the news, as she and Mr. Davis had gotten quite close. I hadn't yet had the chance to process what I had overheard, and by the look on his face, Willy hadn't either. It was going to be a tough week.

The following day, Mr. Davis started taking short walks along the road toward the lumber yard. Momma would link her arm with his, and would stroll with him to make sure he didn't fall, or overwork himself. Momma gushed to us over supper that night about how Mr. Davis had taken over a hundred steps that day.

"He's doing so well!" she exclaimed. "We may make it all the way to the lumber yard by the end of the week."

Unfortunately, Dr. Little's assessment turned out to be prophetic, and Mr. Davis had a stroke the following morning at the breakfast table. It was almost as though he had fallen asleep for a few seconds. He dropped his fork onto his plate with a loud clanging sound, and stared silently at nothing. His eyes were glassy, and a small amount of spittle ran from his mouth. We were all scared, but moments later, he seemed to come to his senses, without even realizing that anything had happened. Momma handed Mr. Davis a towel, and he took it from her, a confused look on her face. She quickly covered her mouth, and excused herself from the table, with tears in her eyes. Pappy carried on with conversation as if nothing had happened, and Willy and I just sat and stared. I could feel a pit in my stomach.

Mr. Davis passed away two days later while sitting in his rocker in the room that Pappy had fixed for him. Momma had been the one who found him, with his open Bible sitting on his lap, and his pipe still hanging from his mouth. Our entire family was heartbroken, and Momma cried uncontrollably for hours in her room.

Albert had written a letter to Momma and Pappy, thanking them for all of their kindness and friendship. Within the letter, he included instructions for his funeral and burial, and had also left instructions with the funeral parlor for his service. At the bottom of the letter, he had written, "*Yesterday's gone, and can't be changed, tomorrow is a mystery that only time can unravel. Love all you can today.*" Behind the letter, tucked into the envelope, was five hundred dollars to cover the funeral expenses.

Dr. Little came to the house to confirm what we all already knew, and to talk to Pappy about what steps to take next.

"It appears he has been dead for no more than two hours," the doctor told him. "I'm putting the time of death at 6:30 a.m. I will send for a hearse promptly."

Dr. Little went back into town, and it wasn't but a few minutes later when an ominous, black hearse drove up the drive, and into the yard, to retrieve the body of Mr. Albert Davis for the funeral parlor. Willy and I watched from our bedroom window as the hearse pulled away, and for the first time that morning, I allowed myself to cry.

A rose, will bloom and then the petals will fall
And the wind will just sweep them away
But the smell of the rose will still linger on
After the flower has withered away.

From my notebook {RC}

22

Burial at Mt. Zion

THERE WAS A MEMORIAL service for Mr. Davis two days later at Mt. Zion Baptist church just off the Amory highway, a mile or so past the Davis farm. It was a small church that sat back in the pines. Pappy, Mr. Purnell, Dr. Little, Mr. Davis's attorney, Justin Webb, his brother, Joe, and his grandson, Peter, were pallbearers. Willy, Momma, Mrs. Purnell, and I sat in the section marked for family. Mrs. Purnell Sang "Amazing Grace," and contrary to what Wayne had said about her singing, she had a beautiful voice. She then read a short poem that his wife had written to him, right before she had passed away, that Momma had found tucked in Albert's bible.

Weep not my love

My heart is thine
My soul will wait for thee
For death is but an Angel's touch
That sets the spirit free

Weep not my Love nor should thee pine
For days that cannot be
For soon our hearts will join again
For all eternity

The Pastor of the little church read some scriptures, that Momma had selected, and said a prayer. He told of the date of his birth and the time and place of his death. The old man was eighty-nine. There were only five or six other people in the church, and I had never seen them before. Mr. Davis was buried between his wife and son in the little cemetery behind the church. He had already set a tombstone for his wife and himself with both their names and dates of birth engraved. The inscription read, "*Death is but an angel's touch that sets the spirit free.*" Momma cried when she read it.

Pappy said he guessed that Mr. Davis had outlived most of his friends and neighbors, and that's why attendance was so low. I felt sad about that, but I was glad that I had gotten the chance to know him.

Pappy had taken off work to handle the arrangements, but returned to the lumber yard as soon as the funeral and burial was over. I knew that he was upset over the old man's passing, but I also knew that he'd never let it show.

"Life goes on," he told me.

It had been several days since Albert Davis had passed away, and Pappy, Willy and I been seeing to his livestock every day. It was starting to turn into a real chore for us to drive out each day after pappy got off work to do all the feeding. Over supper, Pappy told us that he was going to have to talk to Mr. Davis's lawyer about what he was going to do with the farm, because he couldn't keep on managing it himself for much longer. He was off from work on Wednesday afternoon, so he and Momma set up an appointment, and went to see the attorney about the property.

On the second floor of the Simmons Building, at the law office of Justin T. Webb, a well-dressed woman behind a glossy, oak desk greeted them.

"How can I help you?" she asked them with a smile.

"Well, ma'am," AC began, "we are here to see Mr. Webb about the estate of Albert Davis. I called him about a week ago."

"Oh, yes, he's expecting you" the woman informed them. "I'll let him know that you're here. One moment, please."

The woman walked down the hallway, and reappeared a moment later, asking AC and Allie to follow her. She led them back to a private office, lined with bookshelves filled with old law books and files. An older man in a pinstriped suit stood from behind his desk and shook hands with them. He motioned for them to take a seat.

"Now, what can I do for you, Mr. Calloway?" he asked.

"Well, Mr. Webb, as you know, Albert Davis had been staying with us just before he passed, and we have been seeing to his place and livestock since his passing, but we can't keep that up for long," AC told the man. "I have a job to see to, and neither of my boys are old enough to drive. We just wanted to know what plans Mr. Davis had to handle the farm and his livestock. He's got fifty or sixty head of fine Hereford cattle out there, and that takes a lot of seeing after. He also has chickens and hogs that have to be fed daily. We know that his death came suddenly, and we'll do what we can to help until the livestock can be sold, if that is what needs to be done."

Mr. Webb looked perplexed.

"I'm not sure how to say this, Mr. Calloway," he attorney said, leaning forward on his desk. "Apparently, Mr. Davis did not tell you, but he signed that property over to you and Mrs. Calloway a week or so before his death. He also left instructions that you are to inherit all of his possessions, including the cash in his bank accounts. Of course, you will have to go through probate court, and the will reading, but the land and cattle are yours to do with as you please. I was preparing to send you a letter to that effect with complete instructions on the settlement myself, but I had figured that he told you."

AC and Allie Calloway sat in the man's office, utterly speechless.

"Mr. Calloway, you and Mrs. Calloway now own more than twelve hundred acres of land. You are a very wealthy man. I have been Albert's attorney for many years, but was also proud to call him a good friend. I can tell you that Albert also has more than a half-million dollars in government bonds and cash. That part of his estate will be yours in about sixty days. My fees have been paid, as well as all of his other debts, which were mighty few," the attorney went on.

"I hope you will see fit to allow me to be your attorney, too," Mr. Webb smiled. "I'm getting up in years, but my grandson has just finished law school over at Ole Miss, and has just passed the bar exam. I will see to it that he handles your affairs with care, and your business would be strictly between you and our firm. My secretary, Mrs. Kendal, has some papers for you to sign, but essentially, you and your wife will be joint tenants of his bank funds as soon as the will is read."

"This… this is incredible," Allie said softly

"I will send you a letter advising you of the date of the reading of the will," Mr. Webb stood from behind his desk. "You will need to leave your address with my secretary, and if you wish, we can phone as well."

AC stood to his feet, still feeling overwhelmed, and shook the attorney's hand. "Thank you," he managed to say.

"There was one other stipulation to the will that he just added," the man smiled at them, "and that was that your son, Zack is to get his old truck."

"So," AC ran his hand through his hair, "you're telling us that all of that property, and the house, and the livestock is now ours?"

"Yes, sir. That's exactly what I'm telling you," Mr. Webb said. "You can move into the house if you wish. You and Mrs. Calloway own the property now. You can do with it what you want.

"This is going to have to take some getting used to," AC said. "I don't know, for the life of me, why he would leave all of that wealth to us. I haven't ever even owned a single acre of land."

"Well, I suppose he thought you, your wife, and your boys were some of the most honest and caring people he had ever known, and he knew you would manage his property well. As you know, he and his wife had no kin on either side of the family. Your family was the closest thing to a family he had."

AC and Allie Calloway had gone into Mr. Webb's office with nothing to their name but a family and a few dollars in the bank, and came out as some of the wealthiest people in Tupelo. However, nobody even knew it, and that was just the way they wanted it. They didn't know what the future would bring for their family, but their lives had been changed forever. They would have to tell Wayne Purnell, for sure, but hoped it would not affect their relationship, as there was no one AC thought more highly of than Wayne.

23

School with The Mccullough Boys

Mrs. McCullough enrolled her boys in school as soon as holiday break was finished, much to the consternation of Anna, her friends, the other kids in school, and many of the teachers, too. Mrs. McCullough had bought the boys some new clothes and shoes with the money she had gotten from working at the lumber yard, and they no longer looked like highway bandits. They finally looked like they belonged in a school.

It just so happened that Naught was assigned to my class, while Notch was a grade below us. Much to my surprise, Naught took to school very well. He was an eager learner, and was soon near the top of our class. He excelled in math and science, and could read better than most of the other students. He did have a bit of a chip on his shoulder, but was able to keep his emotions in check, and stay out of trouble for the most part. He mostly kept to himself, and had trouble making friends, because most people could only focus on the way he was before he came to school. Anna and I would try to sit with him after lunch sometimes, where we would all sit on the steps and talk, but Anna's friends rarely acknowledged him. Naught liked our teacher well enough, and was eager to please her. Mrs. Shell gave him some extra attention when he first joined our class to make sure he didn't lag behind, and I could tell that he appreciated it.

Often, Naught would stay after school to help Mrs. Shell clean her room, or do any chores she might have. Some days, he and Notch would be waiting for Willy and me, and would walk down to the lumber yard with us to see their momma before they made their way home. Every now and then, they would even go by to see Mrs. Purnell, and would always leave drinking a soda pop when they left, because Miss Bonnie was a sucker when it came to kids.

One day, just a few days after Naught had joined the class, Mrs. Shell's former husband burst into the classroom in the middle of a lesson, and began cursing and threatening to harm her. I got between them, and told him that he had better leave. When he turned his anger toward me, I held my ground, for I didn't aim to allow him to hurt Mrs. Shell. Naught stood by me, followed by the rest of the boys in the class, and we blocked the man from our teacher until the principal forced him from the room. Minutes later, we heard the sound of a siren, and saw two policemen placing him in a patrol car. Our teacher excused herself from the classroom, very distraught from the situation, and the whole class sat in silence until she returned.

Mrs. Shell thanked all of us students who had come to her aid, and I reckon it may have been the first time that Naught had been praised for anything in a long time. He seemed filled with pride over having defended her, and she seemed very pleased with him as well. It's funny how small things can change your opinion people. It was not long before the whole school learned of what had happened that day. Many students saw a different side of Naught that they never knew before. Sometimes, we just have to keep turning pages to find out what is really inside the book, just like Pappy had said.

When I told Momma and Pappy about what had happened with Mrs. Shell, and how Naught had stepped up to help, Pappy commended me for standing up for Mrs. Shell. He then told me about how he believed that people were a lot like like pears.

"The outside peeling is rough and bitter, but once you cut away the rough outer shell, then you get the good part of the pear" he said. "Mostly, they're good and sweet."

I understood what he was trying to say, but I was certainly not under the illusion that the Mccullough boys were particularly good or sweet. I reckon though, that there is plenty of both good and bad in everyone.

24

The Inheritance

ANOTHER THREE WEEKS PASSED before Mr. Webb called to tell Pappy about the date of the will reading, and the finalization of the probate. When Pappy and Momma told Willy and me about how we were to inherit Mr. Davis's fortune, I could hardly wrap my head around it. They told us that we weren't to tell anyone at school about the money, because it might cause us problems. Pappy and Momma had learned that Mr. Davis total cash and bonds was valued at six hundred and ten thousand dollars. Mr. Webb advised Pappy on how to invest the money to reduce the amount of taxes that would be due, but even after taxes, there would be a lot of cash. He said he would teach Momma how to handle the cash to make sure the banks kept it insured, if she wanted, or they could hire an accountant to advise them. Pappy told him that he wanted to talk to Mr. and Mrs. Purnell before they made a decision on any of those matters.

Mr. Webb also told Pappy that his brother, Joe, lived out near the farm if he needed any help on the farm.

"He's got a forty-acre farm himself, and he picks up odd jobs now and then. He's a good hand. Made a ton of money in the banking business, but just up and quit one day. Just walked away and bought that farm. Now, he's happy as a pig in sunshine. He can do about anything with his hands. I'll get his number for you to call if you need his help. He also knows just about everybody in Lee county," he told Pappy. Pappy thanked him and told him he would be in touch with his brother, for he had plenty of work that needed doing on the farm. Pappy said he knew that there needed to be new fences on just about the whole place. Mr. Davis had simply not been able to do much up-keep, and did not seem to have the will to hire it done. There was also the roof on the old house that was in pretty bad shape and would have to be repaired or replaced. It would all have to wait until the will was final though, for they had no cash for that now.

That Wednesday, Pappy was off work for the afternoon, so he and Momma drove directly to the

Purnell's home. They lived in a nice, big house, only a little way from where me and Willy went to school. Pappy parked his old truck at the curb and got out. Bonnie Purnell was on her knees, pruning her rose bushes when they walked up. She wore a wide brim, straw hat, and a bush jacket and she held her hand on the top of that hat as a strong wind blew.

"Afternoon, Bonnie," Pappy greeted her.

Bonnie looked up, immediately recognizing Pappy and Momma. Wayne Purnell was sitting on the porch steps, polishing a pair of shoes. He was in his sock feet.

"What a nice surprise," Bonnie shouted as they approached. "Get your shoes on, Pee, we've got company."

Wayne Purnell slipped his shoes on, and got up to extend his hand to AC.

"You all come on up on the porch and we'll go inside where it's not so cool., as he stood to greet them. Maybe we can get you s cup of coffee." "What brings you over to this part of town? There ain't anything wrong, is there?"

"No, there's no problem," Pappy told him, "but we got something we need to talk over with you two."

Pappy went through the whole story he had just learned from Mr. Webb, while his Momma and Bonnie sat and listened. Everyone was silent until he finished.

"Well, damn, AC. Congratulations, you're a mighty wealthy man," Wayne clapped him on the shoulder. "What you gonna do with all that wealth?"

"Don't know. Never had more than a few hundred dollars in my entire life," Pappy said. "Thought you all might be able to help us with that. Lawyer said it will be a while before we get any of the money, but the farm and house are already in our possession. I'd like for you to drive out there on Sunday and take a good look at the farm. I know there's plenty of work that needs doing, as Albert hadn't been able to do much for a few years."

"Sure thing, AC, we'll drive out right after lunch on Sunday," Wayne said. "Hope you're not planning to leave the lumber yard. Sure wouldn't want you to do that."

"Nope, I've grown to like the lumber business, and the boss man ain't too bad either," Pappy smiled. "So I reckon, if you want me, I'll just keep on working. The boys are old enough now to help me with the farm. I plan to lease out the crop land. Had a fellow that said he'd pay cash rent for the two hundred acres he plans to plant in cotton. The rest we'll need for hay and corn for the animals. Got a plan for that, too. Got another fellow who will cut and bail the hay on the halves, and will pay me a fourth of the corn crop. Should have plenty of feed for the livestock."

"That sure sounds like a plan," Wayne stroked his chin.

"Me and the boys can put up the hay with a little help from the McCullough boys," Pappy went on. "They've turned into pretty fair hands. We plan to let the Mrs. McCullough and her boys move into the house if she wants to. She needs a car, and she can't pay for a car, and pay rent, too. Don't know if she'll want to or not, but we are going to make the offer. She could have a garden, and there's already chickens if she wants them. She's turned out to be a good hand at the lumber yard."

"Well," Wayne said, "I have another idea for you to mull over. There's a mighty nice place for sale just three houses down the street from us. Why don't you go and take a look? You could be our neighbors. Mrs. McCullough could move into the place where you're living. We'd sure like to have you as neighbors."

"Now you're making sense, Pee!" Bonnie exclaimed. "Best idea you've had since you asked me to marry you."

"Now, Bonnie, you know that ain't so. I've had plenty of good ideas. Like hiring AC to manage the lumber yard."

"Well, there was that one," she smiled.

"I don't know, Wayne," Pappy said, turning to Momma. "I don't want to move too fast. Never had any money to manage before. This is a mighty fine neighborhood, but we'll have to think on it."

"Take your time," Wayne nodded.

25

Trip to The Davis Farm

ON SUNDAY, MR. AND Mrs. Purnell came over to the house, and Momma and Miss Bonnie sat on the front porch and visited, while Pappy and Mr. Purnell drove us out to the farm. Willy and I sat in the bed of the old truck, with our backs against the cab, while Squat sat beside us, his nose hanging over the side of the truck bed, sniffing the wind and announcing our coming to every dog we passed. Squat had the longest tongue of any dog in Mississippi, and put out out more slobber than a hydrophobic hippopotamus. The side of the truck looked like we had been through a snowstorm. If Pappy wasn't careful, that hound would soon be riding shotgun in the cab.

Mr. Davis's farm was huge. Pappy drove over the property for nearly an hour before he pulled to a stop in front of the old Davis house. He went to the well behind the house, dropped the well bucket down into the well, and drew up a bucket filled with cool, clear water. A tin dipper hung on the cross-bar that held the well pulley, and Pappy rinsed it out before taking a large swig.

"Mighty good water," he nodded. "I'm going to have to find a plumber to pipe it to the house. The McCullough's will need inside plumbing."

We all took a drink from the bucket, but it just tasted like water to me. Pappy poured the rest of the bucket onto the ground, making a muddy puddle, and Squat began lapping. He didn't know if it was water or whiskey, and likely didn't care. He just liked it. With a tongue as long as he had, he could lap up a bucket full faster than you could pour. Once we'd had our fill, Pappy and Mr. Purnell went back around the Davis house, and took a seat on the front steps. Willy and I sat in the rockers right behind them.

"Been wanting to run a few more things by you, Wayne," Pappy said.

"Well, this is a good time to do it. I've got some things on my mind that I've been wrestling with as well." Mr. Purnell said. "But you go on ahead and tell me what you're thinking first."

"Well, there are a few things I've been thinking on," Pappy began. "The first is that we badly need more warehouse space. We're selling so much bulk lumber now, that we're having to buy partial truckloads to keep up with the demand. That's expensive. We need to be buying boxcar loads at a time. The problem is, we have no room in the existing yard to build more storage sheds. Second thing is, Wayne, this country is changing, and we have no colored people working for the company. We have quite a few Negro customers, and I think I would like to hire a Negro to work in the yard to help with loading and deliveries. I also think you might consider hiring a smart, young, black woman to help out inside. Wouldn't hurt if she was real pretty too."

Mr. Purnell listened closely, nodding his head.

"The black movement is taking hold all over the country, and it may be time we get on board," Pappy went on. "A young black preacher down in Atlanta is leading the charge in the south, and a black lawyer with the NAACP in Kansas has filed suit to have public schools integrated. President Truman is pushing for faster integration of our military services, and is giving his support for the school case in Topeka. I believe it will not be far off until we will have integrated schools all across the nation. It won't be pretty in Mississippi for we've got a whole train load on knuckleheads in the statehouse, and elsewhere, who will resist such a movement with their last dying breath."

Willy and I listened with keen interest for we never knew Pappy knew so much about things that were happening in the world.

"I agree with just about everything you've said, AC," Mr. Purnell replied. "We do need to expand our operation. People are buying television sets left and right, and now we've started selling washing machines, electric cook stoves, and even refrigerators. I need three times the space I've got now. Mr. Thompson, who owns the dry cleaners next door, is getting up in his years. He has talked some about retiring. He's got about a acre of land with his business, and it has frontage on Main street, which would be helpful if he would sell. And there's the pasture land behind your house also. There's probably about twenty acres there, but I don't even know who owns it. I think maybe we should look into it. Would you be interested in partnering up on such a deal if it could be made? We're talking about a pretty substantial investment."

"I think I might be, Wayne, but I would have to talk to Allie about it," Pappy said. "I wouldn't want to make such a commitment without Allie's approval. You'll need to talk it over with Bonnie, too, I reckon. I think we should get the wives together to talk all this over tonight."

"If we can find the room to expand, I reckon it would be a good time to add a couple of new employees as well. I think it would be the right thing to do, and good business to boot. I'll get Bonnie to have some of her real estate connections check into the two pieces of property we just mentioned, and we'll see where that leads."

Pappy nodded, and the two of them carried on talking about business until a chill began to creep into the air.

It was mid afternoon when we piled back into the old truck, and drove back into town. Momma and Miss Bonnie were in the kitchen preparing supper, and Momma gave Pappy a quick kiss when we walked in.

"Thought you boys had gotten lost out there," Miss Bonnie said as we came through the door. "Thought I was going to have to send out a search party."

"Well, we might have been there longer, but Wayne could smell Allie's cooking from the farm, and we just followed that smell all the way to Tupelo," Pappy smiled.

Even though Pappy and Momma had sat us down and told us about the money we had inherited from Mr. Davis, I felt no different about anything. I just missed Mr. Davis. Pappy had said that every now and then you would meet someone, and it was like opening the cover of a new book. He said we could learn lessons from everyone, and that every person had a story to tell, but wc have to keep turning the pages if we really want to get to know a person.

"Most people never get past the title page," he had told me. "and the miss the whole, wonderful story."

I knew that Pappy had a lot of pages to him that I had not turned yet.

26

Willy's Big Announcement

WILLY CALLOWAY SAT ON the bleachers alone with his glove and bat. It was the last day of practice before the first game of the season, and he was glad that he was able to join to experience the first, full season of baseball with the Tupelo High School team. He was good at baseball, and really loved to play, but Willy had another interest that few people knew about, and it weighed heavily on his mind. His Pappy was such a big baseball fan, that he knew that he would be sorely disappointed if Willy did not give his all to the sport, so he was not really sure about how to bring it up to him. As much as willy loved baseball, what he really wanted to do was fly. However, he didn't want to disappoint Pappy.

A captain from the newly formed Tupelo Air National Guard had come to the school to talk to his class about the National Guard, and how it was possible to earn wings through a program that they offered in conjunction with the Air Force base at Columbus. Willy knew that it would be difficult to get into the program, because required rigorous testing, both mentally and physically. He wouldn't be able to apply until he was seventeen, but he was very good at math and science in school, and felt confident that he could handle anything the Air Guard would throw at him. It was nearly a year away, but with his parent's approval, he could join the National Guard at sixteen, and he could begin prepping as he continued his high school requirements.

Willy had been so caught up in his thoughts, that he didn't even realize that his younger brother, Zack, had come to the field, and was getting equipment out of storage. Although Zack was a year younger than him, he was really a smart kid, and he valued his judgement on most things. He would definitely have to ask him his thoughts on it before he talked to Pappy and Momma.

It was nearly dark by the time practice was done for the day. Willy and Zack met up, and started walking home.

"Got something I want to talk to you about, Zack," Willy said, shoving his hands into his pockets. "You can't talk about it to anyone else though, okay? Can you do that?"

"What, did you rob a bank or something?" Zack asked.

"No, I ain't robbed no bank. This is serious, Zack. I'll tell you about it tonight, but you can't tell Momma or Pappy, got it?"

"Well, I ain't getting involved in no criminal enterprise, I'll tell you that right now."

'You know better than that," Willy said. "Shoot, I may not even tell you about it. Not with your attitude."

"I'm just saying, Pappy wouldn't like it much if we ended up in jail," Zack shrugged.

"You know, sometimes I think you have a one-track mind, but then I wonder if you even have a track," Willy sighed.

"Just trying to keep you out of trouble, brother."

"Uh huh, whatever you say."

That night, when supper was over, Willy and Zack retired to their rooms. Willy had moved into the room that Pappy had fixed up for Mr. Davis, and Zack had their old room all to himself. It had taken some time to get used to not sharing a room with Zack, for the two boys were about as close as two brothers could be. Both boys loved school and learning, and were always at the top of their classes when it came to their studies. Being the older brother, Willy often helped Zack if he was having trouble in a subject. Zack was not the athlete that Willy was, but he was still better than most of the boys he competed against. Unlike Willy, who cared little for sports other than baseball, Zack liked to play all kinds of sports, but didn't take any of them too seriously.

Zack knocked on Willy's door, and entered without waiting for an invitation.

"What's going on, Willy?" he asked. "You said you wanted to run something by me."

"Yeah, but you have to keep it to yourself until I can run it by Momma and Pappy myself, okay?" Willy said.

"I can do that as long as it ain't something that's gonna get you hurt or killed."

"No, Zack, it's nothing like that," Willy rolled his eyes. "I'm thinking about joining the Air National Guard when I turn sixteen, so I can learn to fly. I don't know how to tell Momma and Pappy. They've got a program where I can earn a commission and learn to fly, and it's what I really want to do. What do you think?"

"I think Pappy may just kill you himself," Zack said, "Momma might even help him."

"I don't want to disappoint Pappy," Willy said. "I want to play baseball, but I won't be able to put in as much time with it as I know Pappy would like me to."

"Dang, Willy, you've bit off a chunk. I just hope you can swallow it."

"Yeah, I know. I think I'm gonna run it by them at supper tomorrow night," Willy said. "I want you there."

"Where else would I be?" Zack asked. "I'll be there. Haven't seen a boy beat to death with a skillet yet, and momma is likely to do it to you. You might just as well get it out there, since I know you've got your mind made."

The next day was a long one. All I could think about was Willy's dilemma. Anna was absent from school, and her friend, Penny, told me that her mother had taken her to the doctor with a cough and some congestion. I usually spent about fifteen minutes with Anna at lunch time before she went to class, but that day, I played four-square on the sidewalk with Danny Hill and Billy Oaks. It was hard to believe that we were already halfway through the spring semester, and that I would be turning fifteen in just two months. The year was passing quickly, but my mind was consumed by what might happen at the supper table that night.

Tupelo played Columbus in the first baseball game of the season that afternoon. They let classes out early to watch the game at noon. Tupelo won big, finishing 12-2, with Willy leading the team with a single, two doubles, and a home run. Pappy came to watch for his lunch hour, and stayed for the entire hour. Momma stayed for the whole game, and she was so proud. We all were.

When Momma called us to supper that night, Pappy was already seated at the table, and Willy had cleaned himself up, and sat himself down next to Pappy.

"Good game, Willy," Pappy said.

"Thanks," Willy smiled. "It felt good to get started playing again."

Momma piled food onto our plates, and sat them before us. I dug in immediately, forgetting about Willy's situation. Before he even took a bite, Willy cleared his throat.

"There's something I want to talk to the family about tonight before we start eating," Willy said, his face slightly pink.

Pappy and Momma laid down their utensils, and looked to him questioningly. I followed their lead, and laid my fork beside my plate, waiting for Willy to continue.

"Pappy, Momma, I want to join the Air National Guard," Willy said confidently. Pappy and Momma's eyes went wide, and before they could say a word, Willy went on to tell them about the captain who came to talk to his class about the National Guard, and how he had decided that he wanted to join up when he turned sixteen in May, and start training for the officer training when he turned eighteen. "I also want to start my pilot training as soon as I finish OTS. Flying is something I really want to do."

The house was so quiet, you could have heard an ant fart. Pappy's face showed absolutely no emotion, but Momma looked like she had just swallowed a horse fly. Her face turned red as a beet pickle.

"I would have to attend drills at least one weekend a month here in Tupelo, and go for additional training at either Columbus or Biloxi for two weeks in the summer," Willy added. "It wouldn't affect my school work at all, and I can handle both. I just need both of you to sign a piece of paper that says that it's okay for me to join up when I turn sixteen."

"Willy," Pappy finally spoke up, "you do know there's a war going on in Korea, don't you? What if your unit gets called up?"

"Then I'd have to go," Willy said simply.

Pappy, being a thoughtful, deliberate man, was silent for several moments before he spoke again.

"Tell you what," he said. "Let me and your mother mull it over for a day or two, and we'll let you know our decision. Now, let's all eat our supper."

Willy looked content with his response, but Momma looked like she was ready to mull Pappy's head with a skillet. I knew she probably wouldn't be ready to let Willy sign up for the National Guard even if he was forty.

Nearly two days passed before Pappy told Willy about their decision over supper. We had heard Pappy and Momma talking in hushed tones in their room late at night, and even arguing at times. I wasn't sure what to expect, and neither was Willy.

"Your Momma and I are both very proud of you boys," Pappy began. "Well, I guess I shouldn't call you boys anymore, seeing as you've both grown into young men now, and have shown good judgement and character in everything you've done since we moved to Tupelo. Sometimes, it's hard for parents to let go when their children start to show their independence, but it always happens. I will say, however, that we didn't expect it to come this quickly."

"So, you've made up your mind then?" Willy asked.

"Yes, son," Pappy nodded. "We are going to sign for you, Willy. If this is what you want to do, you will have our permission. However, we want to make it known that both your momma and I have reservations about this choice. We'd still like for you to consider going to college, especially as we have the money to send you both, if you want to go."

My jaw just about dropped to the floor. I sat totally speechless, as Willy thanked Pappy and Momma, and promised that he would consider college. Willy was interested in all kinds of aeronautics, and while the National Guard was his first choice, he said he might even consider one of the military academies, if they offered pilot training school. That response seemed to please Pappy and Momma, and they allowed the conversation to shift into other subjects as we ate our supper.

A few days later, late in the afternoon, a Jeep from the guard unit pulled up in our front yard. I guess Willy had told them that Pappy was off on Wednesday afternoons, and that he would be available to talk with them on that day. Two came to our door to talk to Willy and Pappy, and I tried to listen in to the conversation, without being too obvious.

One of the men was an officer named Weeks. He explained to Pappy and Willy all of the things that the National Guard would expect of him, and what Willy could expect from the National Guard. After a while, Momma and I joined the conversation, and the two men spoke to all of us for a good hour. I sat by Willy, and listened as they explained the Officer Candidate School, and the flight school program. They also explained that Willy could not enlist until two months before his seventeenth birthday, and that Momma and Pappy would need to give their consent. Willy looked a little disappointed at not being able to enlist when he wanted, but Pappy and Momma nodded. The men left papers and forms for them to sign, and then left.

When the Jeep had pulled out of the driveway, Willy and I went to his room to talk about what the future held for him, until Momma came to fetch us for supper. Pappy mentioned nothing about the Guardsmen at the supper table. As far as Pappy was concerned, the matter was over and done with. His decision was made, and all that was left was for Willy to sleep in the bed he had made.

27

Building Fences

ONE MORNING, PAPPY TOLD Willy and me that there was a good deal of fencing that needed to be done on Mr. Davis's old farm, and that he would be hiring the McCullough boys to help us. It would be a pretty big job, so Pappy would also be bringing in a local man to oversee the fencing, and to make sure we didn't slack off. I knew that Willy and I weren't slackers, but I wasn't so sure about the McCullough boys. I wondered if they could even tell a fence post from a cow bell. But I was excited about earning some spending money of my own. I wanted to be able to ask Annabelle Owens to go to a movie with me, and pay for her way, too.

Pappy and Mr. Purnell had entered into a business agreement for expanding the lumber yard business, and were able to make a deal on the pasture acreage behind our house, so that they could begin negotiating on the adjoining, dry cleaning property. They agreed that Pappy would purchase the property, and would hold fifty percent in the business. It was also agreed upon that they would form a new cooperation, and call it "Number Six Lumber." Mr. Purnell, his wife, Momma, and Pappy would each own twenty-five shares of stock in the company, and would make up the Board of Directors. Attorney Webb was managing all of the legal details. Mr. Purnell would be president, Pappy would be vice president, and Mrs. Purnell and Momma would share the name of treasurer. Pappy was now a major business man in Tupelo, with a lot on his plate, and always seemed busy doing some sort of work. His dream of returning to farming back in Big Flat seemed to be drifting further away each day.

The school year had flown by, and it was nearly time for summer break. I had turned fourteen just after school had started, and although I couldn't get a permit to drive until I was fifteen, Pappy surprised me by saying that he thought it was time I started studying for my driver's license. I had held on to the old truck that Mr. Davis left me, and I was eager to learn in a more official manner than driving a dying man to town. It would be some time before I could get my permit, but I hoped that Pappy would let me start practicing out on the farm. I couldn't wait for the day when I could take Anna for a drive around the streets of Tupelo.

The last day of school came quickly. I was excited to be out for the summer, but I knew that I would miss all of the friends that I had made, especially Anna. When school was let out for the last time that year, Anna and I said goodbye at the pickup site in front of the school, and she took my hand as we walked. Mrs. Owens was waiting to pick her up, so I knew that there would be no goodbye kiss happening. I told Anna that I would call her as soon as I earned enough money for us to go out to a movie.

"I'll surely miss you, Zack Calloway," Anna said to me. "Don't make me wait too long to see you again!"

On the first Saturday of summer break, Pappy took Willy, me, Naught, and Notch out to the Davis farm to start working on the fencing job. The McCullough boys insisted on riding in the back of Pappy's old truck, and were joined by Squat, who seemed to get along well with them. Pappy let Willy drive the truck, since Willy had gotten his driver's license a few weeks prior to school being let out. Pappy made him drive slowly, but he got us there without Pappy having to correct him too much. When we arrived at the farm, Pappy introduced us to meet the man who would be overseeing the fencing, and showing us what all needed to get done. The man introduced himself as Joe Webb, and I then realised that he was the brother of Mr. Webb, the attorney.

Joe Webb was a tall and lean man with a leathery face, blue eyes and a bush of grey hair. He had a long scar along his left cheek that gave him the appearance of continuously smiling. He was a jovial person and was continuously joking and kidding with the four of us. I liked him immediately, for he was filled with funny stories and seemed to enjoy whatever work he was doing. According to Pappy, he had made a lot of money in some kind of business but was unhappy with being tied to a desk job and had sold his interest in the business and bought a small farm and was now happy and content. He had no wife or children that he ever mentioned but he often talked about his nephew as if he were his own son.

Pappy had purchased a truck load of Creosoted fence posts, fifty rolls of barbed wire, and twenty rolls of hog wire for the job. The wire had been stacked in the tractor shed, right beside the firewood that I had stacked months before. The fence posts sat in a pile out beside the pond, ready to be loaded onto the farm wagon, which Joe Webb had hitched to the old tractor, and distributed by our crew. We were to start rebuilding the fence that ran along the highway first, because it was in the worst shape, and pappy wanted to be sure that the cattle wouldn't get out onto the main highway. This section alone was more than a half mile of frontage.

Pappy handed each of us a brand new pair of Blue Mule leather gloves, and Joe Webb directed us on how to load and unload the fence posts on the trailer. As we began unloading, he and Pappy discussed what parts of the farm was to get new fencing. I found that handling the tar and oil treated posts was a chore, that would make nearly anyone think of making a break for the county line. I was thankful for the leather gloves, because the treated posts burned your skin if they touched a bare spot, and they stunk to high heaven. On top of all that, the strong smell permeated the nostrils, and made it hard to breathe. It hadn't been more than five minutes before the McCullough boys were swearing like seasick sailors. Before the day was finished, Willy and I were both starting to wish that we had finished those boys off with that baseball bat that day in front of the school. On top of everything else, the weather had turned hotter than a blacksmith's cinder box.

"I'll tell you one thing, Hell ain't got nothing on Mississippi," Naught proclaimed as we began unloading the fence post along the line where the new fence would be built. "I think my noggin is plumb fried. Old pitchfork himself probably got his training right here in Tupelo."

The next day, Mr. Webb decided it might be best to separate the McCullough boys, before they started fighting with each other. He put Notch with Willy, and Naught with me. Naught was as strong as an ox, but couldn't dig post holes worth a flip. I worked with Naught all that week, and we got along pretty well. By the end of the week, he had started getting pretty good at digging holes, but he still fussed a whole lot, and swore every time he picked up a post.

"Who invented the dang post hole digger?" he asked me out of the blue.

"I got no idea who invented it," I said. "Probably somebody who was digging holes with a shovel."

"Well, he should have been beat to death with it," Naught swore. "Hardest contraption I ever saw to operate that looks so simple."

"Well, just be careful. You can cut toes off if you don't watch yourself." Naught stopped digging and just looked at me. "It's happened," I said.

"Damn," he said, "I bet that hurt."

"Expect so."

I never asked Naught any questions about his family, but I was curious about what had happened to his father, and if he had any other kinfolk anywhere. We stopped that day about mid-morning to take a short rest break and get some water. Mr. Webb had brought us a jug of ice water, and we both took a drink from the jug, then sat down under the shade of a large a Persimmon tree, with our backs against the trunk.

"I sure like your daddy," Naught said. "He's been mighty good to me and Notch, and our momma. Don't know what we would have done if he and your momma hadn't helped us. We were in mighty bad shape."

"Yeah, Pappy likes to help people," I said, unsure of what else to say.

"My daddy ran off and left us right before school started, and we haven't seen him since," Naught said. "We were living over near Calhoun City then. Momma moved us here so she could look for a job. Calhoun City wasn't much of a town. She mostly cleaned houses for folks. Then she got sick real bad. I reckon Momma is better off without our daddy though. He stayed drunk most of the time, and used to beat her up sometimes. He would beat on me and Notch, too. Momma said she had heard from him only once since he left. He had told her he was in jail down in Texas, and wanted her to send him some money for bail. Momma didn't have no money to send him, so he may still be in jail for all I know. I hope he don't never come back. If he did though I wouldn't let him hurt Momma anymore. I sometimes wish Momma would find herself a good husband. It would be good to have somebody around to show me and Notch how to do stuff like your daddy does," he said.

"You have any other kinfolk around Tupelo?" I asked him.

"No, not around here. Momma has a sister over in Missouri somewhere, but she ain't no better off than we are. She couldn't help us even if she wanted to. When I get old enough, I aim to join the military, if they'll have me. Don't know which branch I'll join yet. Been thinking on the Marines. Maybe I can help our momma then. I'll be giving most of what your daddy pays me to our momma to help with the groceries."

"Why don't you talk to Willy?" I asked. "He's getting ready to join the Air National Guard. He might be able to help you."

"Yeah? I think I'll do that," he nodded.

"Pappy was in the Navy during the war," I said. "Overheard him and Mr. Purnell talking about it one day. They were both there when Pearl Harbor was bombed. That's how they met up. Both of them were injured, and spent time in the hospital at the same time. I heard Mr. Purnell say that he wouldn't be here today if Pappy had not pulled him from beneath a burning Jeep."

"Wow," was all Naught said.

I found a new respect for Naught and his brother that day. I was finally starting to turn the pages in Naught's story, too. It was more interesting than I ever thought it would be. Maybe he wasn't so bad. We went back to digging post holes, and although he was starting to get the hang of it, Naught still swore up a storm as we dug.

At noon on the following Saturday, Pappy picked us up for more work on the fence, and paid us for last week's work. It came out to twelve dollars for each of us. It wasn't much, but I sure felt rich, and I couldn't wait to tell Anna that I had enough money to take her to the movies.

When we had finished the day's work, Pappy told us to go to the fish pond and wash off before we went home. He had brought some soap from the old Davis house, and a few towels to wash up with. Momma and Mrs. McCullough had sent clothes for us to wear home after we bathed. Once Pappy had told us to head to the pond, we had all stripped naked by the time we reached the levy. Mr. Webb told notch to watch out for Octowalrus in the pond, as he winked at Pappy.

"Octo what? Notch asked, stopping in his tracks."

"Octowalrus, Mr Webb stated seriously. Got nine arms like an octopus but looks kinda like a walrus. Walks upright like a person and eats everything in it;sight. They've already run two or three out of that pond. Probably not any more in there.

Notch's eyes were big as saucers and Pappy was about to bust a gut to laugh.

The rest of us couldn't hold it any longer and just burst out laughing as we dove into the water.

The water was ice cold, even though the day had been mighty hot. But we soon got used to it, and were swimming and diving in no time. Notch couldn't swim very well, so he never got far from the levy, but Naught, Willy, and I were all over the pond. I didn't mention that Mr. Davis had said there were snakes in the pond, but I kept an eye out just in case I spotted one. I wondered if that tar and oil that we washed off wouldn't kill every fish in the pond, but reckoned that if it hadn't killed us after a week, it probably wouldn't hurt the fish either.

After about a half hour in the pond, we had pretty much scrubbed ourselves clean. Pappy told us to get dressed, and get into the truck, as it was time to go home. We dropped the McCullough boys off at their house, and Mrs. McCullough waved to us from the porch when Pappy pulled to a stop. I notice that they had cleaned up around the house, and it was starting to look nice. There were curtains on the windows, and a new screen door had been put up. Once we had dropped off the McCullugh boys, Pappy took us home.

28

A Date with Annabelle

MR. PURNELL TOOK THE liberty of having a phone installed in our house, for he said he might need to call Pappy after work hours. I think it was just because he liked Pappy so much, he just wanted him to have the modern convenience. Pappy rarely used the phone, but Momma took to it right off. She called Mrs. Purnell every day, and Mrs. McCullough every night. I was happy that we now had a phone, so I could call Anna, and ask her if she could meet me at the drugstore, then go to the movies. She said she would have to ask her mother, so I waited, holding my breath until she came back to the phone.

"She said yes!" Anna exclaimed. "She said I could go to the three o'clock show, but I have to be home by six, and you have to walk me home."

Hearing that her momma was allowing me to take her out made my day, and I couldn't wait to see her that night.

The Tupelo drugstore was on the corner of Main Street and Broadway, not more than four blocks from my house. It was a popular spot with teenagers and adults alike, and I was excited to bring Anna there. The drugstore had a large mirrored wall behind the soda fountain, with a long, tiled counter, which stretched half the length of one side of the store. Two young women, dressed in white smocks, waited on customers from behind the counter. There was a menu above the soda fountain, and shelves filled with medical supplies and household goods covered the walls. Chrome tables with red tops, and matching, padded chairs, stood in a line against the far wall.

The drugstore had only a few customers when I walked through the door, and it was easy to spot Anna, who was already there, seated at one of the tables. I felt my eyes widen, as I took in how pretty she looked. She wore a black skirt, with a white blouse, matching black and white shoes. She smiled when she saw me, and I waved, walked over, and sat down across from her at the table. She reached over and touched the back of my hand, and I felt my nerves settled a little. I noticed she was wearing the locket I had given her for Christmas, and smiled.

The drug store was one of the few stores in Tupelo that had air conditioning, and it was certainly nice to come into after working in the sun all week. I didn't have a clue what to talk about with Anna, but I was glad to see her. I wanted to touch her, but didn't know if I should.

"I've never ordered a milkshake before," I said to her. "In fact, I don't think I've even had a milkshake before. What do I do?"

"Well," she smiled, "do you like chocolate or vanilla?"

"I guess I like both," I told her.

"So do I," her eyes sparkled. "So, just walk up and tell the girl behind the counter that you would like to order a milkshake, and tell her what flavor you want, and then tell her that you'd like two glasses and two straws."

I did just as Anna had instructed, and a few minutes later, one of the women in white brought out two glasses, and a large, chocolate milkshake in a tin cup.

"That'll be fifteen cents," she said, holding out her hand.

I paid her a quarter, and told her to keep the change. Momma had told me to always leave a tip for the people In eating places that served the food. The girl smiled and thanked me. Anna poured the shake, filling both our glasses. I took a sip through the straw. It was cold and delicious. In fact, I don't think I had ever tasted anything better.

"My goodness, that's good," I said. Anna just smiled and took a sip.

"Yes, it is. Thank you. You did good ordering the shakes."

"I don't know much about how to act in a town like Tupelo," I told her. "We didn't have anything but two stores and two churches in Big Flat, so I've got a lot to learn. I hope I don't embarrass you by doing something foolish. If I do something wrong, just tell me. I have to warn you, I've never bought a movie ticket before either. Pappy took us to shows at school a few times, but he always bought the tickets for us. You may need to help me. They showed movies at the school during the summer in Big Flat, but they didn't use tickets. They were mostly old cowboy shows."

"Don't worry about embarrassing me, Zack," Anna said reassuringly. "You're doing just fine, but if you want my help with city ways, just ask. I've lived here all my life."

"Thanks, Anna."

"The movie starts at three o'clock, so we'd better get going," Anna said as we finished up our milkshakes.

It was a warm, Saturday afternoon, and the streets of Tupelo were crowded. White and black people alike were doing their weekly shopping, and the stores on the main streets were alive with activity. Tupelo was very much a segregated city. There were drinking fountains for white folks, and separate ones for blacks. There were few places for black people to buy lunches for themselves, and no restaurants where they were welcome to sit with whites. The courthouse square was a gathering place for farm folks for both business and socializing. The Lyric Theater was on the corner of Broadway and Court Street, and we could see the marquee well before we got to the theater. "*The Quiet Man*" was showing, with John Wayne and Maureen O'Hara. There was already a crowd gathered beneath the marquee waiting to buy tickets. I had never seen a John Wayne movie, or anything with Maureen O'Hara, but Anna knew all about them both. She was overjoyed when she saw the marquee.

We got in line to get tickets, and she held onto my arm the entire time. It felt good having her beside me. It took a while to get the tickets, but we finally entered the glass doors to the lobby. The smell of popcorn and hot dogs cooking was about more than I could stand, and I realised then that I was as hungry as a plow horse. I asked Anna if she wanted something to eat and drink.

"Maybe just a Coke," she said.

I got in line, and ordered us two Cokes, and a bag of popcorn.

"Got to have some popcorn," I said. "We can share."

"I'd like that," Anna smiled.

We entered the theater and took seats near the middle, for all the seats up front was taken. I didn't care where we sat, as long as Anna was beside me. There was a balcony above that was filled with negros, and I wondered why they got the best seats in the house. The lights turned down, and music filled the theatre as the movie began to play. It was a very long movie, and we both laughed a lot as we shared the large bag of buttery popcorn. It was so good, I could have eaten the sack myself, had Anna not been there.

When we walked out of the theater, it was well after five o'clock and Anna had promised her mother that she would be home by six. We quickly crossed Broadway to Court Street, which took us by the county courthouse. It was an impressive, domed structure, and the plaque on the street informed those passing by that it had been built in 1909. It sure didn't look like it was that old. There were magnolia trees planted around the courtyard and a statue of a soldier faced the street. Anna wanted to sit on one of the benches for a while, which was just fine with me. The crowd had mostly thinned out, now that it was late in the day, and things finally felt calm.

We sat for just a short while, while Anna told me all about what it was like growing up in Tupelo, and how much she enjoyed living there. Her love for the town was obvious.

"I just love this town," she sighed happily. "I don't know if I could ever be happy living anywhere else."

"I like it, too, but sometimes I really miss Big Flat. Someday, I think I want to go to college to study medicine. I want to be a doctor, and I want to have my own farm, too. I love living on a farm and being around animals. Most animals have better dispositions than people," I said. Anna looked at me strangely, like she was seeing something for the first time. "What do you think? Is that a crazy thing for me to be thinking about?"

"No, it's not a crazy plan at all," she said. "I actually want to be a children's doctor someday. But if the right person asked, I might become a farmer's wife, too. But I know nothing of animals or farming."

"Don't you worry," I said. "I could have you slopping hogs and milking cows in no time flat." I laughed, and she punched me on the shoulder.

"We'd better get going," she said, standing up.

Just as we were getting ready to head toward her house, a black panel truck pulled up to the curb in front of us. The truck had "*Mississippi Slim and The Kentuckians*" painted in big, white letters on the side. A small man got out of the truck, and walked over to us.

"You kids want to earn a couple of tickets to the show tonight? All you've got to do is help me take these instruments up to the courtroom on the second floor. I've got a live radio show here tonight at eight. Good country music and comedy. I'll give you front row seats for a helping hand," he offered.

"Sure," I said, taking the two tickets.

"Here," he said, handing two more tickets, "invite a couple of your friends. They call me Mississippi Slim.

You can just call me Slim if you want to. My real name is Lee Ausborn. Been performing mostly up in the Detroit area lately, but we're going to have a special radio show here tonight. Used to play here every week."

I had heard of the Mississippi Slim, and had even listened to him on the radio, but never had I imagined that I'd ever meet such a famous person. We helped him with the equipment up the stairs, and he thanked us graciously.

"I hope I'll be seeing you all tonight!" he said, before driving away in the truck.

"Well," Anna said turning to me, "that was sure something!"

"Yeah," I nodded. I couldn't wait to tell Willy about meeting the Mississippi Slim.

The sun had began to set as we made our way toward Anna's house, casting shadows across the town from behind the trees. Anna took my arm, and pulled herself close to me as we walked. It was all I could do to restrain myself from taking her in my arms and kissing her right there. I knew, however, that Annabelle Owens would let me know when she was ready for that to happen, if ever it did. Besides that, I didn't know much about kissing, and figured I'd probably bloody her nose or something.

"Reckon your mother would let you go to that radio show?" I asked.

"I can ask," she said.

"I sure would like to go to that show," I told her.

Anna lived in a nice neighborhood. There was a small magnolia tree on the east side of the lot her house sat on, and there were flowers planted along the walkway to the steps, and crepe myrtles beginning to bloom on the east side of the house. The houses, she explained, were mostly newer homes, which were built for servicemen returning from the war. She told me that her father had been killed at Normandy. He had been a soldier by choice, and had intended to make the Army his career, but was severely injured during the landing, and he died a few months later. Her mother had purchased the house with the military's insurance settlement. They had been staying with her grandparents, who lived just out of Columbus at the time, until her mother was, through a friend of the family, offered a job at the bank in Tupelo. She had started out as a teller, but was now head of the accounting department. I could tell that Anna was very proud of her mother.

We made it to Anna's house just before six, and Anna invited me in to meet her mother. When she said I needed to meet her mother, I just about took off running. I hadn't thought about having to do that, but I gathered my courage, stuck my hands down deep in my pockets, and followed Anna inside. As soon as I saw Mrs. Owens smile, it was plain as day where Anna got her beauty; she was a spitting image of her mother.

"So, you must be Zack?" she greeted me extending her hand.

I took her hand and shook it. "Yes, ma'am, I am. It's nice to meet you. Anna talks about you a lot."

"She does, does she? And you call her Anna, do you?" Mrs. Owens raised an eyebrow.

"She has told me a lot about you. It's crazy, because I had no idea that a mother and her daughter could look so much alike," I said. "You look like you could be sisters."

"Oh, aren't you sweet!" Mrs. Owens smiled again.

"I try, ma'am," I said. "And, yes, I do mostly call her Anna—hope you don't mind that." She smiled and nodded her head, which I took to mean that it was okay, but she didn't answer. It was like she was going to give it some more thought.

"Why don't you and Annabelle go to the living room and sit, and I'll get you some iced tea, or maybe some lemonade?" her mother said.

"No, thank you, ma'am, I have to go. Pappy told me to be home by seven, and Pappy is strict about us being home when we're supposed to be there. Anna and I were given tickets to the Mississippi Slim radio show tonight at the courthouse though. Would you mind if Anna came with me to see it? I've got to get approval from my pappy, of course."

"I don't know, Zack, you two have practically spent the whole day together."

"We've got extra tickets," I said without thinking. "You could go with us if you wanted to. We wouldn't mind at all, would we Anna?"

"No, of course not." Anna said. I heard the words come out of her mouth, but I could tell by the look in her eyes that it was not at all what she had in mind. I was definitely a greenhorn when it came to understanding women.

"That's alright, Zack," Mrs. Owens said. "Thank you for the offer, but I'll have to politely decline. I give you my permission to go with Annabelle tonight, if your father approves, that is." Anna looked relieved at her mother's words.

"Yes, ma'am," I said. "Thank you."

"Annabelle, why don't you walk Zack out to the porch?"

"Of course," Anna nodded. "Come on, Zack. I'll walk you out."

I followed Anna out to the porch, and she ask me to sit for a moment in the porch swing with her. I sat down beside her, and she took my hand, held it to her heart, and looked into my eyes in a way I had never seen before. I felt weak.

"Do you believe in God, Zack," she asked. "I need to know."

I was caught off my guard by her question. I had never been asked that question before—by anyone. Not even my parents.

"I do," I told her. "I reckon I've always believed, but until recently, I guess I never considered that there are people who don't." We had gone to church nearly every Sunday when we lived in Big Flat, but had not been since we moved to Tupelo. Pappy didn't seem too interested in church since we had moved. "Why do you ask?"

"I don't know, Zack, it's just a feeling I have, like he's always near me, and I pray for you every day," she said. "I pray that God will protect you, and that he will allow you to love me. I just feel like he has something special in store for you, and for me, too."

"I've never prayed much, but I have asked him to protect you, and that you won't ever find some boy that you like more than me," I told her.

"Thank you for telling me that, Zack. I hope you are not mad at me for asking. Momma says some people get upset if you ask about their religion."

"I've never been mad at you, Anna, and I don't ever plan to be. I've got to go now, but I'll try to call you as soon as I can."

"Oh, before you go, I didn't tell you, but tomorrow I'll be going to Columbus to stay with my grandparents for a while—might be two or three weeks."

"Two or three weeks?" I asked. "Why so long?"

"My mother has to go to school in Jackson for new things they're doing at the bank, and she'll be gone for two and a half weeks. I will be with my grandparents until she gets back home. I don't want to go, but I don't really have a choice in the matter. My mother has to go to keep her job at the bank, and she won't leave me alone for that long."

"I don't blame her for that," I said. "I'm sure gonna miss seeing you, and knowing you're close by."

"You go now, and call me if you can go to the radio show tonight."

I got up to leave, and Anna put her arms around me. She laid her head on my chest, but did not kiss me. She just held me for a moment, and then said goodnight, and went inside. My mind felt cluttered again as I made my way home. I was thinking about Anna leaving, and God, and the future, and Willy joining the National Guard, and Mississippi Slim, and building fences. I hated it when I had too much to think about. My brain wasn't equipped for deep thought like that.

That night, I had to call Anna from Mr. Purnell's office, and tell her that Pappy wouldn't let me go out again. We'd have to catch the show at another time, if it was still around when she got back from staying with her grandparents. I was a bit disappointed that I wouldn't be seeing her again before she left. I told her that I'd give the tickets to Willy if we couldn't go, since he had been wanting to ask Jessica to go out, but hadn't got the courage yet. Anna seemed surprised that Willy would want to go out with Jess, but

"I know Jess likes him, too" she told me. "I never thought he would like her. I bet she would go with him."

29

The Hospitalon The Hill

OVER THE NEXT SEVERAL weeks, we found ourselves digging more post holes on the farm. Naught and I dug, while Willy and Notch helped Mr. Webb stretch out some barbed wire, and staple it to the posts. Pappy was putting up five strands, about eight inches apart. It was a fine fence, strong and straight as a string from one corner to the next. Along the highway, Pappy was using hog wire, with three strands of barbed wire above the hog wire. Pappy wanted a good fence along the highway. He said he didn't want any cows getting out on the road and causing a wreck. There wouldn't be any weak points in the fence we were building.

Naught continued to fuss and moan about the work, but he was building muscle, and getting browned by the sun. He had lost all of the fat around his midsection, and he was proud of his new appearance. I had toughened up, too, and had grown another inch over the last few months, but I was rail thin, and not muscular like Naught. I couldn't seem to gain any weight, even though fence building caused me to eat like a hog. But I was strong, and was now a bit over six feet tall. I was taller than Willy, and Pappy, too.

Willy and I toiled the whole summer on that farm, and I saw very little of Anna. I was actually looking forward to being back in school, because at least I would see her every day. We talked every week by phone, but I didn't like to talk to Anna on the phone. I wanted to see her, and look her into her eyes. However, the last two or three times I that called Anna, no one answered the phone. I wondered why that was, and I figured that maybe she had gone back to Columbus to stay with her grandparents, but I thought she would have told me if that were the case. I just couldn't imagine why she had not called me. I sure hoped she wasn't mad at me about something.

It was seven o'clock by the time we got home from the farm, and had eaten our supper. I had asked Momma if it was alright if I called to check on Anna, and she said I could, but told me she thought I was too stuck on that girl. That I was too young to have a really serious relationship with a girl. I listened to her, but Anna was so special, I just didn't feel ready to tell my Momma how much I really cared for her.

I was still seated at the table when the phone rang. Momma was up, so she answered it. She said hello, and listened, before turning to me. "It's for you, Zack."

I stood and took the phone from Momma, expecting Anna to be on the other end. But it wasn't Anna's voice that I heard. It was her mother's.

"Zack, you need to listen to me," she said, her voice cracking slightly. "Annabelle is very sick, and she wants to see you. We are at the hospital now. We've been here for nearly a week now. If you can come, I will do my best to explain what's wrong when you get here. She's very sick, Zack."

"I'll be there as soon as I can get there," I said. Mrs. Owens said nothing more, and all I heard next was the *click* of the line going dead.

Momma and Pappy had been watching me from the table, and they could immediately tell that something was wrong.

"What is it, son?" Pappy asked.

"Annabelle is sick," I said, swallowing the lump in my throat. "She's in the hospital. I have to go to her. She wants to see me."

Pappy nodded. "Go get cleaned up. I'll take you as soon as you're ready."

I took a quick bath, put on clean clothes, and met Pappy back in the kitchen.

"We need to hurry," I told him.

The hospital in Tupelo was not a new structure. It was built in the 1930s, in the midst of the great depression, with money from Eastern investors, and a pricey sum of $35,000, which had been raised by local citizens. It was built for facility, not beauty. It was a long, rectangular building, three stories tall, with no distinguishing feature other than a broad portico, with four colonial columns at the entrance. The hospital had fifty beds, and was known locally as the "hospital on the hill". It was one of the best equipped that Mississippi had to offer.

Pappy pulled up in front of the building, and told me to go on in and find Anna's room, and that he would find a place to park the truck. I went through the front doors, and was immediately hit with the smell if antiseptic and alcohol, reminding me of when Mr. Davis was here. The front doors opened into a waiting room and admitting area, and a sign on the counter read "Information." I asked the lady behind the counter what room Annabelle Owens was in. She looked on a clipboard and said, "She's in the ICU."

"What does that mean?" I asked.

"Intensive Care Unit, third door. You'll need to check at the nurse's station up at the waiting area. The elevator is right over there," she said.

"I've never rode on an elevator," I said. "How does it work?"

The lady smiled. "Come on, I'll show you. Where are you from?"

"Well, I'm from Tupelo right now, but we ain't been here long enough for me to get acquainted with elevators. I was here at the hospital once before, but we never went past the first floor. We moved here from Big Flat," I told her. She didn't act like she knew where that was, and didn't seem to care much.

"I have to wait on my pappy," I said. "He's parking the truck."

I know she had heard me, but she kept walking. When she got to the elevator, she showed me the buttons, and explained what to do. I waited there for Pappy by the elevator as the lady returned to her work station. When he finally came through the double doors, he saw me, and I motioned him in my direction. I pushed the button to get on the lift, and when we were inside, I pushed the button for the third floor. Pappy seemed to be about as knowledgeable as I was about elevators, and he held on tightly to the handrail as the box went into motion. It was a little unsettling for us both.

"Never cared much for elevators," he said. "I'd rather climb a rope."

We got off on the third floor and turned left. An arrow pointed toward a sign that said "ICU", and we kept going. We stopped at the nurses station and asked if we could see Annabelle Owens. The nurse told us to wait, and that she would check with Mrs. Owens.

She disappeared through another set of double doors, and was gone for only a moment before returning. Mrs. Owens walked beside her. She was visibly upset. Her eyes were red, and her hair had not been brushed. She looked years older than when I had last seen her. She walked straight to me, and put her arms around me, hugging me tight. I could feel her shaking, and I was suddenly very scared.

"Zack, Annabelle is dying," she said to me, pulling away. "She has cancer. Colon cancer. The doctors say that it's advanced, and that there is no cure for what she has, and that she probably only has a few weeks, or perhaps only days to live."

"What? No, that can't be true," I said, as I took Mrs. Owens by the shoulders and held her away from me. "How can this be possible? She's only fourteen." I felt a burning in my throat, and tears forming in my eyes. "Can I see her? Please?"

"Yes," Mrs. Owens answered, her voice hoarse. "They have just given her a blood transfusion, and some more medication. She usually feels better for a little while, but it doesn't last but a few hours, and she can't have another until tomorrow. She wants to see you. She's been asking for days for me to call you, but the doctors said she absolutely could have no visitors. But today, however, they relented. The cancer is taking over her body, and there's nothing that can be done. They said that she could have visitors if she wanted. You may be shocked at her appearance, Zack—she has lost a lot of weight, and her eyes are very dark underneath."

"It's okay, Mrs. Owens," I said to her. "I want you to know right now that I love Anna, and I want to stay with her for as long as she has. Will you take me to her now?"

Pappy was standing by, listening intently as we talked, and I suddenly realized that I had not introduced him to Mrs. Owens.

"Pappy," I said, turning to him, "I want you to meet Anna's mother, Mrs. Owens."

Pappy smiled, and reached his hand out to her. She took it, and said something that I didn't quite hear, for my thoughts were on Anna. Mrs. Owens told Pappy that she would take me to Anna's room, and would come back and get acquainted right after. I was glad that I was going to be alone with Anna for a while, for all I wanted to do was kiss her, and tell her how much I loved her. I didn't know how I was going to make it without Anna. I couldn't wrap my mind around her dying.

"Are you ready, Zack?" Mrs. Owens voice snapped me back. She led the way back through the double doors toward Anna's room in the Intensive Care Unit.

The ICU area was not large. It was a narrow room, and had cubicles on each side of a nurses station. The cubicles had no doors, but were curtained off from the station. At each end of the unit was a room with large, plate glass windows, and an entrance door. These rooms were for the most critically ill patients. Anna occupied one of these rooms. There was a single chair beside her bed, but no other furniture.

Nurses could monitor the patients in these rooms through the large glass front. The window, however did have a curtain that could be drawn to shut off the light when Anna was trying to sleep. There area was not a quiet place. There was lots of activity and machines running all the time and people talking constantly. I wondered how anybody could ever sleep with all the noise. There were chalkboards outside each room with the name of the attending physician and attending nurse. There were also telephone numbers for emergencies. Mrs. Owens number was on the board and right below hers was my name and phone number. I held back tears.

We reached Anna's room, where there a nurse was tending to Anna, who was sitting upright, propped on a pillow in her bed. She smiled widely and held out her arms for me. I accepted her invitation, and gathered her in my arms. She was crying, and clinging to me as if she would never let go. I sat down beside her, and she kissed me, just as she had on the day I had given her the locket.

"Oh, Zack, I'm so glad to see you. The doctors wouldn't let me have visitors. But I guess they think it doesn't matter anymore. They're saying I'm going to die, Zack. I just can't believe what's happening to me."

Her voice was weak and raspy, but she clung to me with all her strength.

"You can't die, Anna. I love you, and we've got things to do. We've got medical school to go to, and I've got to teach you to milk cows and slop hogs," I told her.

Anna laughed through shallow sobs, but she didn't let go. She clung to me, and then kissed me, caressing my face with her hands, as if to make sure it was really me. I didn't want her to let go either. I could feel her warmth, and I felt her body tremble, as though she were freezing cold. It nearly broke my heart.

30

Staying The Night with Anna

ANNA HAD TUBES RUNNING to her arms, and she was connected to a machine that had all kinds of numbers and lines running across a screen, which looked a bit like a tiny television.

"What is that machine?" I asked.

"Newest thing, they tell me. An oscilloscope. It's supposed to read my heart rate, my blood pressure, and who knows what else," Anna told me.

"Oh, Anna…" I said, unsure of what to say.

Anna took both my hands in hers, and looked at me directly. "Zack, I want you to stay with me tonight,"

"That's what I came to do, Anna," I squeezed her hands. "I'll stay here for as long as you want me here."

"No, Zack, you don't understand, I want you to stay the night with me—lay with me, and make love to me, and hold me. I want to make love to you," she said, a bit of pink touching her pale face. My jaw about dropped to the floor. "I've talked to my mother, and although she protested plenty, she finally gave her permission for you to stay. Nobody will interrupt us through the night. We will have our privacy, and my mother will be guarding the door. She is going to tell your father, and she is very persuasive," Anna smiled weakly. "I want to be the first girl to make love to you, Zack. You are my first love, and the only boy I have ever kissed. I don't want to die without experiencing that part of love, too, and I don't ever want you to forget me."

"I love you, Anna," I said, "and want to make love to you, too. I would never forget about you, but this ain't like buying a milkshake or movie tickets. I have never even kissed anyone but you, and don't know anything about having sex."

"We'll learn together," she said. She pulled me close to her, and kissed me. "I don't know much either, but I made momma talk to me about it some once before, but she started crying, and she finally said I would figure it all out in time."

I don't think that Anna's mother knew that sex was part of Anna's plan. I knew for sure that Pappy didn't. He'd probably drag me out of Anna's room by my ear. She held me for a long time more. She was surprisingly warm, and I figured it must have been because of a fever. I cupped her face in my hands, and kissed her. I knew my Pappy would not approve of what we were about to do. I also knew that if my momma ever found out, she'd likely slip into a coma.

I was still holding onto Anna when her mother knocked on the door, and entered the room with a nurse.

"Annabelle, the nurse is going to remove the IV until morning," she said, eyeing us.

"I'll be back in first thing in the morning to replace it," the nurse smiled. "If you need a shot for the pain, just press your button to let us know."

"You two have until seven o'clock to spend together," Mrs. Owens said to us. "Annabelle, please call if you need anything. No funny business."

She came to the bedside, and kissed Anna's forehead, before embracing me in a tender hug. She left the room, and left us alone. I was alone with Anna, and for the first time, I felt a deep fear come over me. Would I have to watch Anna die alone? I wasn't sure if I could handle that.

"Come here, Zack," Anna said softly.

I sat beside Anna on the hospital bed, and she moved to one side and invited me to lay beside her. I kicked off my shoes, and stretched out beside her. She turned on her side to face me, and pulled me to her, where I could feel her warmth through the thin hospital gown she wore. After a moment, she shed the gown, and lay beside me completely naked. Light from the window cast a dim glow over the bed. The room was mostly dark, with the only other light came from the scope above Anna's bed. The only thing she wore was the locket that fell between her bare breasts. My heart was racing.

"Nice locket," I smiled at her.

"You sure you're looking at the locket, Zack Calloway?"

"Maybe not altogether," I laughed. "You're beautiful, you know."

She kissed me again, pulled me to her, and unbuttoned my shirt. I soon lay naked beside her. She pulled me to her, kissed me again, and I moved on top of her. Our love making was clumsy and awkward, but it didn't matter. I loved Anna, and I felt that she really loved me. Our love making continued until Anna was exhausted from the activity. She then turned on her side, her back to me, and pulled my arm around her. I was not sure how long I could lay with Anna like that without wanting her again.

"I have to rest now," Anna said softly. "I may wake you later though."

"I'm praying that God will make you well, Anna" I said to her. "I believe He can do that. If he knows how much I love you, he would surely do that, right?"

"I don't know if that's how it works or not," she said. "I'm thanking Him for bringing you to me, and allowing you to love me. I guess what we've done here tonight is sinful to some—maybe even to God. But I don't feel like it is."

Her sentence trailed off, and she slipped off to sleep. Anna's breathing was soft and peaceful as we lay together.

Hours later, I eased from the bed, and put my pants, before sitting in the chair beside the bed. I rested my head by Anna, and took her hand in mine. I wondered if this night would be the night that Anna would die. I didn't know what I would do if that happened. It was like Anna had now become a part of me, and I felt changed forever. I didn't think my heart could stand the pain of losing her. I had only known her for a few months, but it seemed as though she had been there my entire life. Sleep finally overtook me, and I dreamed of Anna and me at the movies, and walking together down the streets of Tupelo.

31

Dr. Luke Appears

IT WAS WELL AFTER midnight when Anna and I were awakened by the glow of a light hovering over her hospital bed. There was a man standing over us, and the light seemed to be coming from a band around his head. Even with the light, it was difficult to see his face in the dark. Anna quickly covered herself with the bedsheet in surprise, still naked, for we thought we would be alone until morning.

"I'm sorry, Annabelle, but I need to prick your finger for a blood sample," the man said. "I also need give you some medication that will make you feel much better. My name is Dr. Luke."

"Oh, okay," she said, as she extended her hand to him.

The doctor pricked Anna's finger, felt her pulse, and caressed her temples. I then watched as he gave her a capsule of some sort to take with a sip of water. He took a tiny sample of Anna's blood and with his finger, and touched the center of her forehead with the blood. It was hardly big enough to see, and before I realized it, he had come around the side of the bed, and also touched my forehead with Anna's blood.

"Sorry I had to interrupt you," Dr. Luke said, "but this will make you better." He then leaned down, and whispered into my ear, "Anna will live."

The light went out suddenly, and the doctor was gone. I blinked in the darkness in confusion. It felt almost as though I had been dreaming. Anna had already drifted back to sleep, unphased by what had just happened, and I soon joined her.

Anna woke me at six o'clock, with a quick kiss on my lips.

"You have to get fully dressed. My mother will be in in a little while," she said, holding my face in her hands. "I don't know why, but I feel much better this morning."

"Want me to guess?" I smiled, making her giggle.

I took another look at Anna's beautiful, naked body, held her for a moment, and kissed her once more, before pulling my shirt on.

"Zack, tell my mother to come in here, would you? I'm starving, and I know you must be, too," she said with a sly grin.

"I am pretty hungry," I said.

"I'll have my mother order both of us some breakfast from the cafeteria."

"You don't have to do that. I can wait."

"No, I want you to have breakfast with me."

I did as Anna asked, and found Mrs. Owens sitting in a cushioned lounge chair just outside the door, reading a magazine. She looked as though she hadn't slept a wink.

"Anna's hungry, Mrs. Owens," I said. "She wants you to order her some breakfast."

"What? She has barely touched food in nearly a week," Mrs. Owens said, standing up. "They've been feeding her through a tube."

We walked back into Anna's room together, and I was shocked to see Anna sitting up on the side of the bed. She had slipped her hospital gown on once again.

"What are you doing sitting up like that, Annabelle? You know the doctors said you need to lie down and rest," Mrs. Owens protested.

"I feel fine, mother, but I'm starved. I want some eggs and toast. Oh, and bacon. And, oh yeah, I want some juice and jelly. Bring Zack the same thing, he's hungry, too," Anna told her mother.

"I can pay for mine, Mrs. Owens," I began to say.

"That won't be necessary, Zack. Breakfast is on me," Mrs. Owens said with a hint of a smile. I guess she was feeling relieved that Anna was finally willing to eat.

It seemed like forever before breakfast came, and I was feeling about ready to eat my chair. Mrs. Owens asked me to leave the room so she could help Anna to the bathroom, and I took the opportunity to use the men's room in the hallway, and stretch my legs. Our meals came, and we both ate everything on our plates. Anna was sitting up and chattering all the while, as her mother watched in silent awe.

"My goodness, Annabelle, you must be feeling much better. I can't believe you ate all that food!" she exclaimed.

"I feel good, mother. The medicine that doctor gave me last night must be working. I don't feel sick like I have been."

"What doctor, Annabelle?" Mrs. Owens raised her eyebrow.

"Dr. Luke. He came in a little after midnight, took a blood sample, and gave me a pill to make me feel better," Anna told her. "It must have worked."

"What are you talking about, Annabelle? There was no doctor that came in last night. I sat by that door all night, and I can assure you I did not sleep. No one came in after I left the room."

"Yes, Mrs. Owens, there was a doctor that came in. See that spot that's on Anna's forehead? That's Anna's blood. The doctor did that. He also put a spot on mine, too. It happened, alright."

I did not tell Anna's mother the rest of the story immediately, as I could already see the panic in her face over the idea that someone had come into her daughter's room without her noticing. She didn't believe it had happened. She pushed the button by Anna's bed to call for a nurse, and within seconds, a nurse came through the door.

"Hello," Mrs. Owens said tensely. "Who is the Dr. Luke that came into the room and gave Annabelle medication last night?"

"Dr. Luke? Mrs. Owens, there's no Dr. Luke that practices medicine here. To my knowledge, no other personnel came into the room last night, by orders of Dr. Little and his nurse," she said. "They must be mistaken."

"Well, my daughter says there was a Dr. Luke in here last night, and so does Zack," Mrs. Owens said sternly.

The poor nurse looked hopefully confused as she flipped through Anna's chart, unsure of what to tell her. I thought it was time I told Mrs. Owens what else the doctor had said, so I asked her if I could speak to her out in the hallway.

"Of course, Zack," she said, following me out the door.

In the hallway, I faced Mrs. Owens. "Mrs. Owens, the doctor we saw said something else, too. He whispered it to me before he left."

"What did he say, Zack?"

"I didn't want to tell you in front of Anna, or the nurse, but he whispered to me, and told me that Anna will live. That's all he said, and then he was gone. It wasn't a dream either. He pricked Anna's finger, and put the blood on both of our foreheads. We both immediately went back to sleep right after."

"I'm calling Dr. Little," she said suddenly. "There has to be some explanation."

We returned to Anna's room, and Mrs. Owens ordered the nurse to get Dr. Little and Anna's Oncologist up there immediately.

"Somebody was in this room last night and gave my daughter something. I want to know who it was, and what he gave her," she demanded.

The nurse nodded and quickly left the room and was gone for only a few minutes, before she returned. "I talked to Dr. Little. He has ordered a blood sample, just as a precaution, to see if she was given her anything that will harm her. They will do toxicology tests in the lab, but blood samples will also have to be sent to a lab in Birmingham for a thorough test, and that will take at least three days to be sure there is no poison in her body."

"Poison?" Mrs. Owens covered her mouth.

"Yes, ma'am, just a precaution."

Now they had me scared. What if someone had poisoned her? What if they thought I Had done something to her? A little while later, we were joined by Dr. Little, who came into the room with another man by his side. The man's name tag said his name was Dr. Brown. He went to Anna immediately, and began checking her eyes, her mouth, and turned her head from side to side checking for swelling. He checked her heart rate, and blood pressure, then proceeded to check her from top to bottom, even her feet. He examined the blood spot on both of our foreheads, and asked the nurse to order tests specifically for the blood dots. Dr. Brown told Mrs. Owens that he saw no indication of anything that would be dangerous to Anna, but that they would have lab results back from our lab by noon, and they would know more then.

"Until then," he said, "we are going to have a nurse with her at all times. If there are changes in her condition, we will be here at the hospital, so that we can give her immediate attention."

This seemed to relieve Mrs. Owen's anxiety somewhat, but she still looked worried. Meanwhile, Anna didn't seem worried at all. She was sitting on the side of the bed now, brushing her long hair. I sat down beside her, and she quit brushing and smiled at me.

"Is it okay if I have a bath?" Anna asked the doctors.

"I don't see why not, if you feel up to it," Dr. Little said. "Your mother or the nurse must assist you, however.

You're still a very sick young woman, Annabelle, and although you're feeling better now, we are going to have to keep a close watch on you."

"I'm going to call Pappy while you're in the bath," I told Anna. "I want to go home and wash up myself, and then I'll be back right after."

"Okay," Anna said. "Hurry back."

Pappy had gone home for the night after talking to Mrs. Owens, and he had to pick me up in front of the hospital.

"How is she?" he asked me as I climbed into his truck.

"You wouldn't believe me if I told you," I said, unsure of where to even start.

Pappy drove me home, where I quickly bathed and put on some clean clothes. I had told Pappy about the mysterious Dr. Luke, and about how Anna was suddenly feeling much better, but not much else. He seemed at a loss for words to explain it, too.

It was a little after noon before I returned to the hospital. Anna had bathed and brushed her hair, and I noticed immediately that some of the darkness from under her eyes had gone. She was propped up on a pillow in her bed, with her mother sat beside her. They were talking and smiling, and I figured that was a good sign. Mrs. Owens had also brushed her own hair, and put on a little makeup. She looked much improved from the night before. They were both beautiful women, even when the were not at their best, but it made me feel good to see them both feeling better. For the life of me, I could not understand why a girl as pretty as Anna would be attracted to a plain boy like me, but I was thankful.

32

The Discovery

Dr. Little, Dr. Brown, and two nurses came to the room around one o'clock, just as Anna was finishing her lunch. Dr. Brown was a no nonsense kind of doctor, and wanted to get straight to the point. He went straight to Anna, and told her that the nurse was going to have to get more blood samples from her.

"We've got the results from our lab here, and there's no indication of any toxins in your system, but we are very limited in what we can do here," he said. "We will have to wait for Birmingham to call for the rest of the results. However, there is something very strange with the sample we took this morning, so we want to run some more tests."

Mrs. Owens looked worried. "Strange? What do you mean?"

"Well, Mrs. Owens, it appears that, as well as having no indication of toxins, there also appears to be no cancer cells in her blood either."

"No cancer?" Mrs. Owens collapsed onto the bed. "How can that be?"

"Well, it can't be. That's why we must do more testing," Dr. Brown said. "We did analyze the blood on Anna's forehead, and it is A positive, the same as Anna's. We have no idea who came into the room last night and gave Annabelle medication, and that's troubling, but it appears she is doing well. We are going to watch Anna closely. We will be back to check on Annabelle around six this evening. Annabelle, you take it easy for now. You can walk up the hallway with assistance if you wish, and there is going to be a nurse in the room with you for the next twenty-four hours." He looked at me and nodded. "Looks like you have plenty of help." He smiled and left the room in a rush, his long, white coat twirling around his knees.

Three days later, the doctors got a phone report from the lab in Birmingham. The report showed no traces of any known toxins, and no indication of any cancer cells present. The lab administrator said he would be mailing a written report that same day. Dr. Little and Dr. Brown were astounded by the report. They ordered the medication for Anna to stop, and also ordered a complete physical examination by a local gynecologist.

I didn't know what all a gynecologist did, for sure, but I knew it had to do with women problems, so I asked no questions, and made no comment. Pappy always said, "If you're not sure what to say, it's probably better to just keep quiet. Don't step in a cow pile if you can walk around it." So, I kept quiet.

The morning after receiving the initial lab results from Birmingham, Dr. Brown and Dr. Little sat in a small office on the first floor of the Tupelo Medical Center. They stared at three sets of x-ray negatives over a lighted screen. The pictures clearly showed the cancerous masses from when Annabelle Owens was first admitted to the hospital. The second set were negatives from Memphis, from the second week after Annabelle was admitted, and showed that the mass had spread throughout her intestines, and into other organs, and had also spread to the descending aorta. There had been no doubt in their minds that the cancer was consuming her. However, the x-ray taken just the afternoon before showed no sign of a mass. The cancer had disappeared. It couldn't be, yet it was.

"What is your professional opinion, Dr. Brown?" Dr. Little asked, shaking his head.

"Well, I want to call another specialist friend of mine in Atlanta, but I doubt he'll be able to shed any light on this case. If not, then it is my recommendation that we send the girl home, apologize to the mother for making the wrong diagnosis, and never mention it to anyone. If the press got wind of this, they would certainly pester Mrs. Owens and her daughter to no end. I suspect that they would give you and I plenty of grief, too. We can't destroy the x-ray negatives though. I think we have witnessed a damn miracle here, and we can't even tell anyone."

"Mrs. Owens is certainly not going to be happy with us. Hopefully her anger will be tempered by her elation that the cancer is gone," Dr. Little hoped.

"I agree, but it doesn't make me feel good to lie to her," Dr. Brown added.

"What do you make of the blood on the forehead thing? What do you think that means?" Dr. Brown asked.

"Well I have heard of ancient rituals where blood was used in wedding ceremonies as a sign of uniting two people as one, and of course in ancient Egypt when the blood of a lamb was used in the Passover, Doctor Little answered. Other than that, I haven't a clue."

The two doctors left the room and took the elevator to the ICU. When they entered the room, Annabelle Owens was sitting on the side of her bed, chattering with Zack Calloway, and her mother. Dr. Brown went to her bed and asked her to lay down on her back. He began to press on her stomach. He asked if it hurt, and she said no.

"We are going to let you go home, after Dr. Carson has examined you, Annabelle. She is on her way here now. It appears as though our initial diagnosis was incorrect. There is no cancer present in your system that we can detect. We just want to be sure that Annabelle has not been harmed in any way by whomever came into the room. We also want you to come in weekly for blood tests for the next month or so. The nurse in my office will set the times for you so that you don't miss any school," Dr. Brown said.

"We are still looking into who the person was that came into Annabelle's room, but it doesn't look promising that we will learn his identity. The lab also showed no unusual strains of medication in her system, so we may never know," Dr. Little added.

Mrs. Owen's could not find the words to express her feelings. She was overwhelmed with relief, anger, confusion, and worry. Hopefully, time would provide them with the answers they sought.

Dr. Carson, the resident gynecologist at the Tupelo Medical Center, finished her examination on Anna while I sat in the waiting room with Willy and Anna's friend, Jess. Willy had taken a real liking to Jess, and she, like Anna, was pretty and smart, and way out of the league for a Calloway boy. However, it was plain as day that Willy definitely had a deep interest in her. It was funny how quickly a girl could change your perspective on everything. Willy had been so totally focused on school sports and flying, but now he had another interest that demanded his attention.

"How's she doing?" Willy asked.

"Dr. Brown said she could go home as soon as her last examination was finished. He said there was no cancer, that they had made a misdiagnosis. That's hard to believe though. Two days ago, they were positive she was going to die, and now she is not even sick. How can that be? It's almost like divine intervention or something," I said, running my fingers through my hair. "I guess the important thing is that Anna is okay. I imagine that Mrs. Owens will have plenty to say to the doctors after she has a day or two to think about it. What a mess."

33

Anna Goes Home

When Dr. Carson finished with her exam, Mrs. Owens came out to the waiting room and told us that Anna was fine, but she was not going to have any more visitors that day. She told me, in no uncertain terms, that I was not going to spend another night with her daughter. I simply nodded my head, for she seemed irate. We were getting ready to leave the waiting room, when Jess's mother came in to pick her up. Willy watched her leave, and we followed them out to the area where Willy had parked my truck. We climbed in the old truck, and started for home. When we came by First Baptist Church, I told Willy to pull over and park. I had something I needed to run by him.

"Let me guess," he said, "you robbed a bank or something?"

"Very funny," I said. "No, it's nothing like that."

"So, what is it?"

"You know how I stayed at the hospital that night with Anna?" I asked.

"Yes, I know. You thought Anna was dying."

"Well, yeah, but there's more to it than that," I said. "A lot more, actually."

Willy raised an eyebrow, and with a deep breath, I told him the whole story about me sleeping with Anna, the mysterious doctor, and the disappearance of her cancer. I don't think Willy heard anything after I told him that I had sex though. There was a look of pure shock in his eyes.

"You had sex with a dying girl? What to hell were you thinking? She probably wasn't even in her right mind," he exclaimed. "Well, I know she wasn't in her right mind if she had sex with you! With all the drugs she was probably taking, and the pain she has been through, she must have been completely out of it. And what was her mother thinking, allowing you to stay like that?"

"I know how it sounds, Willy, but it seemed like the right thing to do at the time. It was her dying wish. To make matters worse her lady doctor is going to know that Anna has had sex. It might cause problems for the doctors, and for the hospital. If that happens, everybody in Tupelo is going to know, and Anna's reputation will be ruined, and probably her doctor's, too. To top it all off, Mrs. Owens is mad as a hornet, and may not ever let me near Anna again. You got any suggestions?"

"Fourteen years old, Zack" Willy rubbed his eyes. "You know if Momma and Pappy find out, you may not make it to fifteen. You better pray too that Anna isn't pregnant. Damn, brother, you got yourself in a pickle! I got nothing. I never kissed but one girl, and I've never even been close to having sex. Probably just better shoot yourself."

"Yeah, I thought of that, but I'd probably miss myself with a twelve gauge," I sighed. "You think I should tell Pappy? He knows I spent the night in the room with Anna, but he doesn't know the rest of the story. Dang, what a mess."

"It'll be hard, but I think you ought to tell Pappy," Willy nodded. "But I don't think I'd tell Momma right now."

"No kidding! I probably wouldn't need a gun to kill myself if I told her!"

"He's not going to be happy with you, that's for dang sure, but I'd rather have Pappy beside me in a time of trouble than anyone else I know."

We drove home in silence, but my mind was buzzing like mad. I loved Anna, but I felt as though I had somehow betrayed her. I had prayed for God to cure Anna's illness, but I had not asked for his forgiveness for having sex with her. I wasn't sure I even wanted forgiveness. I felt kind of like I had let everyone important to me down, too. It was over with, and I would have to deal with the consequences of what I'd done. I was sure there would be a price to pay for what had happened. But whatever happened, I hoped it would not bring shame to Anna.

Anna was discharged the following day, but her mother wouldn't let her take my calls for the next two days. Willy, the McCullough boys, and I went back to our fence building on Monday, and Pappy asked the other boys to ride in the back of the truck so that he could talk to me alone. He drove in silence for a few minutes, but then asked if there was anything I needed to talk about. I said there was, but that I wanted to think on it today and talk to him when we were alone. It was a long story, and I knew that he was going to be plenty sore at me.

"Well don't let it fester," he said. "It's like a splinter in the butt, and it ain't getting better until you get the splinter out. The sooner you deal with the problem, the sooner the sore begins to heal."

Pappy was right, as usual, and I knew it. I would start dealing with it as soon as I was ready to, but I needed to see Anna first. Unfortunately, I didn't hear from Anna all week. By Saturday, I had made my mind up that I was just going to go to Anna's house, and plead with her mother to let me see her. I did not know if Anna had told her about us having sex, but if she had, Mrs. Owens would probably shoot me on the spot.

34

Legal Problems

ANNABELLE OWENS WAS LYING across her bed with the shades drawn. She had cried every day since she left the hospital. Her mother would not let her call Zack Calloway, and would not let her speak to him when he tried to call her. Dr. Carson, the gynecologist at the Tupelo Medical Center, had told her mother that she had most certainly been sexually active within the last few days, and her mother was starting to suspect that Dr. Brown had been the one who violated her, as he was the only doctor that they could confirm was on the floor that night. If she told her mother the truth about she and Zack having sex, she was afraid that she would never let her near him again. She wanted to ask God to forgive her, but was not sure she wanted to be forgiven for what she had done. She just had to talk to Zack, and she prayed he would come to her.

Pappy picked us up from the Davis farm a little after noon, and bought us all burgers and drinks from little café on the way back into town. We were all as hungry as bears, and each ate two burgers a piece, along with a big plate of fried potatoes. We drove back into town a little after one o'clock, and Pappy dropped off the McCullough boys before pulling into the lumber yard.

"Willy, go on ahead and drive the truck home," Pappy said. "We'll be along shortly."

Willy looked at me questioningly, and I shrugged. He got into the truck and made his way home, while Pappy and I went into Mr. Purnell's office. Pappy shut the door, and motioned for me to sit down.

"What is it?" I asked him.

"We need to have a talk," he said, taking a set on the corner of the desk. "There has been some trouble happening at the hospital here in town, and rumor has it that you may be involved. Now, Zack, I need you to tell me everything, and don't leave anything out."

I looked down at the floor, unsure of where to start. After several moments of silence, I began telling Pappy the whole, lurid story about how Anna and I had slept together in her bed, and about her request to have us make love, thinking that she only had a few days to live. I left out none of the details that I could recall.

"I see," Pappy shook his head. "Well, from what I hear, there's been plenty more developments. Some of the rumors are that Dr. Brown, her Oncologist, may have molested her. If that rumor gets around, it could ruin his career. There is also the rumor that you may have raped the girl while she was in a medicated state. That, too, is a serious charge, and could have long-term effects on both you and Anna."

I was shocked at his words. "What do I do, Pappy? I don't want to be the one to get anyone in trouble over something that I did. I didn't force myself on Anna. I love her. I would never hurt her in that way."

"I believe what you say, son," Pappy said, "however, it's gonna be up to you and Anna to resolve this. If the police get involved, it may get worse before it gets better."

I told Pappy that I wanted to go see Anna today, but that I was sure her mother would let me in the house. He agreed that I should, and asked me if I wanted him to drive me over to talk to her mother.

"No, I've got to think on some things," I told him. "I think better when I'm alone. I need to fix this myself."

Pappy nodded, picked up his old, faded fedora, and placed it firmly on his head. We left the lumber yard, and walked down to the house in silence. Momma was waiting in the kitchen when we walked through the door. I didn't know what Pappy had told her when they were alone, but she never mentioned anything about what Pappy and I had talked about, so I figured she was still in the dark.

It was mid-afternoon when I began walking to Anna's house. There was a westerly wind blowing through Tupelo, and the U.S. flag and the Mississippi state flag waffled in the warm, afternoon breeze in front of the courthouse as I passed. I had planned what I wanted to say to Anna and her mother before I left home, and was determined to maintain my courage to say it. Courage, however, is a strange quality. It's plenty easy to garner when you're only imagining a situation, but it seems to evaporate when the danger is actually faced. The closer I came to Anna's house, the more my resolve wavered.

When I neared the Owen's house, I could see Mrs. Owens in the driveway, washing her car, while Anna sat on the steps of the porch. I was almost to the drive, when Mrs. Owens saw me. She dropped the water hose she was holding, and threw a sponge in the water bucket beside the car. I half expected her to wrap the hose around my neck and choke me to death, but she just stood there, staring at me. I froze.

"What are you doing here, Zack?" she finally asked.

Anna hadn't noticed that I had been standing at the foot of the drive, but when she heard her mother say my name, she looked up, and then began running toward me.

"Get back on the porch, Annabelle," her mother warned.

"No, mother, I will not!" Anna put her hands on her hips. "We need to talk to Zack about everything that is happening. He is my best friend, and he deserves to know all the trouble I've caused."

"Is he also your lover, Annabelle?" Mrs. Owens asked.

Anna stopped dead in her tracks, unsure of what to say. She took a deep breath, and turning toward her mother, "Yes. Yes, he is, mother. I'm not ashamed to say it. But only that night at the hospital. That's the only time we have done more than hold hands. I thought I was dying, mother, and so did you. I never intended to do anything like that before I got married, but I didn't want to die not knowing that part of loving someone. I love you, mother, and I'm the same Annabelle that I was before, and Zack is the same boy as he was before. I'm not a whore like you seem to think I am. I'm just Annabelle Owens, who made love to the boy that I love. We never meant to hurt anyone."

"Oh, Annabelle," Mrs. Owens sighed, shaking her head. "I didn't mean to make you think that you are a bad girl. I suppose I was more angry with myself for allowing Zack to stay with you that night than I was with you. I feel like I've have failed you. I should have used better judgement. Tell you what, let's go inside, and we can sit and talk about this. We've got a lot of things to get resolved before some people really get hurt, and it's only you and Zack that can fix this problem."

That was the same thing that Pappy had told me just before I left him, and I knew they were both right. We went inside to sit at the kitchen table, and Mrs. Owens poured each of us a glass of lemonade. Anna sat beside me and took my hand. She looked at me and smiled. Mrs. Owens took a chair across the table from us. She looked tired.

"Okay, well," Anna started, "thanks for coming over, Zack. I know it took a lot of courage for you to come here. They are accusing Dr. Brown of abusing me. We know it's not true, but he was the only doctor on that floor that night. They say there was no Dr. Luke and the hospital, and the authorities don't believe what we told them that happened. I can't explain it either, and I don't know what else to do but go to the police and tell them the truth, and hope that they believe us."

Mrs. Owens then explained that there was also the possibility that other charges could be filed against me.

"What kind of charges?" I asked.

"Well, at least one of the detectives that's investigating the situation believes your story," Mrs. Owens said. "Unfortunately, he also believes that you raped her, Zack, and that you ought to be charged with rape of an incapacitated patient. That's a very serious charge."

"Oh, no," I felt my stomach knot. "I have to tell my parents, and I have to do it now. Pappy knows some of the story, but Momma knows very little. They have to know all of it. They need to know that we love each other, and that I would never do anything to hurt her. I wouldn't."

"I know, Zack, and we will go with you. I only met your father once, but he seemed to be a good, understanding man, and I know he loves you. I want to hear what he has to say," Mrs. Owens said, standing from the table.

We left immediately, and Mrs. Owens drove us to my house. I felt like my heart might burst right through my chest, I was so afraid. When we drove into the yard, Momma and Pappy were sitting together on the porch swing. We got out of the car, and I mounted the steps first. I quickly made the introductions, and Momma offered Anna and her mother a seat in the two rockers on the porch.

"Zack, go and get another chair from the kitchen," Momma said.

"Actually, Momma, I think it's best if we go inside to talk," I said. "We've got something important to talk over with you and Pappy."

Momma and Pappy exchanged concerned glances, and followed me into the house. As we all sat down around the kitchen table, Mrs. Owens spoke up.

"I'm also sure Zack has told you about Anna having been diagnosed with colon cancer, and how the doctors said it was most certainly terminal," she began. "X-rays had shown that the cancer had progressed to the inoperable stage. They were certain she had only days to live. Once they had made their determination, they told Annabelle that she could have visitors, and she asked to see Zack. They have both been very much smitten with each other, but, according to them both, they had only kissed once. When Zack had given her a locket for Christmas, and nothing more than holding hands after that. Until…" she hesitated, looking to Anna and me "Until that night at the hospital."

Momma turned the color of a collard green. I figured that she knew there was a lot more coming. Pappy said nothing, and his facial expression never changed.

"Once the doctors had told us that they could not operate on Anna because the cancer had metastasized to the descending aorta, and her other organs, Annabelle begged me to allow Zack to stay the night with her in her room, so that they could say their goodbyes, and have some privacy. Against my better judgement, I consented, and told the doctors that I did not want them disturbed. I was naive to think that two, smitten teenagers could be left alone, and I take responsibility for that. That night, while I sat outside the door, Annabelle invited Zack into her bed."

I looked at Momma, who looked as though she just might explode at the thought. She stared, unblinking, as she took in what Mrs. Owens had just said.

"Mrs. Calloway," Anna spoke up softly. "I am so sorry for the trouble I've caused. I thought I was dying, and I wanted Zack to know how much I loved him. I hope you can understand that. I don't think I'm a bad girl, and I know Zack is in no way a bad boy. If I was going to die, I wanted Zack to remember me forever."

"Anna, I surely don't think you are a bad girl, and I will not judge you for what you did," Momma sighed. "Without being in your shoes, how can anyone say what they would do? Loving someone makes us do foolish things, even when we have all our wits about us, much less in a state such as you were in. Now, what else is going on? I know that you would not be here if there was not a lot more to it than you've just told me."

Mrs. Owens went through all that had transpired at the hospital, updating Momma and Pappy on the whole ordeal. She told them about the strange doctor that we had seen, and the disappearing of the cancer from Anna's body, and what the police detectives were saying about Zack, and the possibility of what might happen to Dr. Brown. She told them just about everything.

"I know very little about legal matters," Pappy said, "but I know someone who does." He took out his wallet and found the card that Dr. Little had given him for Mr. Davis's attorney. He went to the hallway and dialed the number. He spoke in hushed tones with the lawyer for a few minutes, then came back into the room, where the rest of us has been quietly waiting. "Well, I caught Mr.

Webb in the office, Pappy said, and I briefly explained our troubles. He said he might be able to help. He said for us to come on over, now!"

Ten minutes later Pappy parked his truck in front of the Webb law office. Mrs. Owens parked right beside him, and we all entered the office together. Mr. Webb was waiting for us and held the door for us when we went in.

"This is my grandson, Pete," Mr. Webb said, introducing us to his grandson, as we entered his office. "He graduated from Ole Miss Law School last May, and has just passed his bar exam. He will be working with me in this office as soon as we can find him some work space. I took the liberty of filling him in on the problem we face. Come Monday morning, we will start trying to get this matter resolved. Today, however, I want to know all the details of everything that has happened. Pete will talk with officials at the hospital, as well as the doctors and nurses that treated Annabelle. I will talk with the chancery judge about getting all parties together for a private hearing. If we can arrange such a meeting, hopefully we can find a resolution without charges being filed against anyone. I do want to say however, Mrs. Owens, that if charges are filed, that you may have some liability in this matter as well. We will just have to see."

Once more, Anna and I told our story, allowing the lawyer to know everything that had happened that night. Pete was sitting in the corner, writing down everything we said, and Mr. Webb also made a few notes on a scratch pad. When we had finished, Mr. Webb told us that they would begin working on the case immediately, and would call us the next week if he was able to set a meeting with the chancery judge. We left the office, and I said goodbye to Anna.

"I'll call you tomorrow, try not to worry," I told her. With Pappy having involved Mr. Webb and Peter, I felt pretty good about our chances of getting the issues resolved. She took my hand and squeezed it as she turned to leave.

35

The Hearing is Set

By Monday morning, we had gone back to the fence building. It had turned hotter than blue blazes outside, and we had to take regular breaks from the heat, which slowed our progress significantly. However, we were getting close to finishing the project that Pappy had laid out for us, and we were all happy about that. Pappy had brought in another thirty heads of Herford brood cows, as well as a huge bull, and now had close to a hundred heads of fine looking cattle, and had enough good pasture for at least that many more. I also asked if Willy and I could work together that week, because I wanted to fill him in on all that had taken place on Saturday and Sunday. He spent Saturday afternoon with Jess, and on Sunday, he had gone to Columbus with a National Guard Captain to tour the Air Base. He had missed all the happenings of the weekend. Since he had gotten his driver's license, he was gone as much as Pappy would allow, so we had not had much time to talk.

Working with Willy was a real pleasure after working with Naught McCullough for several weeks, as Naught's constant complaining had been wearing on my last nerve. Willy and I worked well together, and we made good progress on the fence. However, the worry about the events at the hospital was consuming my thoughts. I wanted the whole thing to be resolved, but I worried that, somehow, it might affect my relationship with Anna, and I sure didn't want that to happen.

Pappy came to pick us up at the farm a little after six o'clock. Mr. Webb had let us off work at five and we had headed for the pond, and were still swimming when Pappy pulled into the yard. We got dressed, and were getting ready to climb into the back of the truck, when Pappy told Willy and me to get up front, because he wanted to talk to us. He asked me if I had told Willy about what was going on, and I told him I had.

"Well," Pappy said, "I got a call from Mr. Webb today, and he has set up a meeting with the chancery judge for Thursday. The judge has also asked that the doctors and nurses that treated Annabelle at the hospital be present. He said he wants to see all medical records, including x-rays and blood tests. Mrs. Owens has already signed a waiver to release the records to the judge. Mr. Webb's grandson, Pete, was able to get the names of all the people involved. He also talked with the chief of police, and learned quite a lot about what they are planning. None of what the police want is good for Zack."

"Anna's input will be crucial," Pappy continued. "The lead detective wants to charge Zack with rape, and I think the judge is just trying to keep the lid on all of this before a lot of people get hurt."

We drove the rest of the way home without more conversation on the subject, but I was starting to get really worried. I knew that if I was charged with such a crime, I could kiss medical school goodbye, and maybe college altogether. I might even lose Anna. Who would want to marry a convicted felon? I couldn't let that happen.

We arrived at the courthouse first thing in the morning, and took the wide, spiral stairs up to the second floor. We were met at the top of the stairs by a deputy security officer, who led us down a hallway, past the main courtroom, and then down another hall, until we were at the rear of the courtroom. He stopped at a doorway that opened into the private chambers of Justice J. Vance Harper. There was a small, outer room with file cabinets, and three small secretarial desks. Nameplates indicated they were for a receptionist, court recorder, and records clerk.

The receptionist was a pleasant looking lady, a little on the stout side, with greying hair rolled into a tight bun. She introduced herself, then led us down a short hallway and into the judge's chambers. It was a spacious area, and some twenty-five or thirty chairs had been arranged in a semi-circle around the judge's desk. Judge Harper sat behind a large, mahogany desk in a padded, leather chair. I looked around at the walls, which were lined with law books, certifications, and pictures. The judge didn't indicate that he even knew we were in the room. Mr. Webb, and Pete were already seated beside the judge's desk, in deep conversation. Soon, Anna and her mother came into the room, and Anna took the chair beside me. She smiled and squeezed my hand reassuringly, but it was plain that Anna was as nervous as I was.

"You scared?" I asked.

Anna nodded.

"Me, too, but we'll get through it."

I had a lot of confidence in Mr. Webb, but even I wasn't sure he would be able to clear up the mess I had gotten us into. It was the first time I had ever been inside a courthouse, except once or twice in Oxford, when I had gone into the courthouse basement to use the toilet. It was unfortunate that I had to be in such a building under such unfortunate circumstances.

The Hospital staff that the judge had summoned came in next, with Dr. Little, Dr. Brown, several nurses, and another doctor I had never seen before in their ranks. Finally, the chief of police, another officer, and finally the Lee County sheriff came in and took their seats. At 9:30 sharp, the judge rapped his gavel a time or two to get everyone's attention. The hearing was in session

36

The Hearing Begins

"I HAVE CALLED YOU all here this morning to try to clear up a situation that occurred at the Tupelo Medical Center earlier this month," Judge Harper began. "This incident was brought to my attention by attorney Justin T. Webb, who most of you likely already know. Mr. Webb has practiced law here in Tupelo for nearly fifty years, and I have known him for at least forty of those years. His reputation and honesty are exemplary, and I believe he will be able to shed light on this issue, and hopefully we can all leave here today in agreeance. I will let him to explain what we know thus far, and we will hear from the involved parties afterward. I want to remind everyone here that what is said here today will be kept within these walls. Mr. Webb, you have the floor."

Mr. Webb stood and gave his head a nod toward Judge Harper. He was a very deliberate man, and it was clear that he was a practiced and skilled orator. When he moved to approach the floor, he took off his suit coat, and folded it neatly across the chair in which he had been sitting. He reached for the gold chain hanging from his shirt pocket, and pulled out a gold watch, glancing at it momentarily before tucking it away.

"Ladies and gentleman, I am going to tell you a story today that has been told to me by Miss Annabelle Owens, and Mr. Zack Calloway. Parts of this story may test your rationale, as well as your religious beliefs, but I ask that you keep an open mind, and listen to what these two, young people have to say. Later, I will give the other parties involved an opportunity to tell you their side of this surreal story. I will also open the floor for questions at that time. I respectfully ask for your complete silence, aside from the person who has the floor." Mr. Webb looked around the room, as the other individuals nodded respectfully, prepared to listen.

"The story begins on the second day of July of this month," Mr. Webb began. "On that day, Annabelle Owens, was admitted to the Tupelo Medical Center with severe abdominal cramping, which had been getting progressively worse over the course of several days. Dr. Little was the family doctor who admitted Annabelle, and subsequently examined her, and ordered x-rays and blood samples. Dr. Little told me that, at first, he suspected a bowel obstruction, or perhaps an infection. However, tests and x-rays later confirmed that this young woman's pain was being caused by something much more severe."

"It was at this time that Dr. Little called in Dr. Donald Brown, an renowned, well respected Oncologist here at the Tupelo Medical Center. Dr. Brown recommended that Annabelle Owens be sent to Baptist Hospital in Memphis for further screening. Miss Owens, subsequently, was transferred by ambulance the following day to Baptist Hospital, where the medical staff immediately began additional testing. On Friday, Dr. Little and Dr. Brown received the call confirming that Annabelle Owens had inoperable colon cancer, which had already spread throughout her body. It was the opinion, of all the doctors concerned, that Annabelle's condition was terminal."

"At this point," Mr. Webb continued, "Annabelle was returned to Tupelo, where she could be near friends and family, and where the hospice process could begin. It was also at this time that Annabelle and and her mother were advised of Annabelle's condition. Further tests and x-rays were ordered, and all came back the same. Annabelle Owens, at the young age of fourteen, was dying. Her doctors, knowing that there was nothing more to be done, agreed that Annabelle could be allowed visitors, and Mrs. Owens allowed Zack Calloway to visit her daughter, who had been pleading and begging to see him so that she could say her final goodbyes to the boy she loved."

"Zack and his father, AC Calloway, arrived at the hospital on Saturday evening. This is when Mrs. Owens, informed Zack about Annabelle's cancer, and the severity of her situation. She took Zack straightaway to see Anna in the Intensive Care Unit. She left the two alone so that she could speak to Mr. AC Calloway, and it was at this time that Annabelle tearfully asked Zack to spend the night with her."

"Now, we've all been young and in love at some point in our lives. Annabelle Owens, believing that she was going to die, as informed by her doctors, wanted to use her final hours to show the boy she loved just how much she loved him, and he wanted to do the same for her. Mrs. Owens, wanting to fulfil her daughter's dying wishes, asked that they be left along for the night, so that they could say their goodbyes. She did not, however, give them permission to have intercourse, nor did she believe it to be possible in Annabelle's dire condition."

"Mrs. Owens then took a chair just outside her daughter's hospital room, and prepared to spend the rest of the night there. That night, believing that she was dying, and wanting to show her love, Annabelle Owens invited Zack Calloway into her bed, and the two teens proceeded to have consensual intercourse. There was no wrongdoing," Mr. Webb paused, as a ripple of whispers spread through the room. My face felt hot, and all I wanted to was shrink away and hide. I looked over at Anna, who looked as though she was going to be sick.

"Judge Harper, I'd like to request a short recess to confer with Mr. Calloway and Miss Owens, if that's alright," Mr. Webb addressed the judge.

"Yes, I'll allow it," Judge Harper said. He rapped his gavel, and announced a fifteen minute recess.

"Come with me, you two," Mr. Webb approached Anna and I. "I want to go over a few things before we return."

Anna and I, as well as our families, followed Mr. Webb and his grandson into a room behind the judge's chambers. I was feeling nervous, but everything that Mr. Webb had said to the room thus far had been true, and I hoped that the others believed it as well.

"Before we continue, I need to know for sure you want me to relate the rest of your story exactly the way you have shared with me," Mr. Webb eyed us. "I should tell you, there are going to be some that will not believe the story about this Dr. Luke individual who showed up that night. Authorities still have not located him, and that is a problem for your story."

"But the story is true!" Anna exclaimed.

"I believe what you say is true, but if the police choose not to believe you, then they may want to bring charges against Zack for that night," Mr. Webb said. "Annabelle, you were on a lot of medication for pain management while in the hospital, and some believe that you were not in the right mind to consent to having intercourse. If that was the case, then what occured can be construed as rape."

"We came here to tell the truth, Mr. Webb," Anna said defiantly, "and the truth is that I invited Zack into my bed, fully in my right mind, and asked him to make love to me. He did not rape me. And as far as Dr. Luke is concerned, how else do you explain the disappearance of my cancer? Something happened that night that cannot be explained."

"Very well," Mr. Webb nodded. "We will continue just as we planned."

Judge Harper tapped his gavel a few times and called the courtroom to order. "This hearing is now in session."

Mr. Webb took the floor again, and just as before, took out his pocket watch for a quick look before beginning.

"Before the recess, I told you a story involving two, young people, hopelessly in love, who believed that one of them was dying. These two young people participated in a consensual, mutual act of love, and are now being punished for it. However, I now wish to tell you about something far more troubling than two teenagers lying together. That same night, Annabelle Owens and Zack Calloway both witnessed a strange, unknown man, come into the hospital room, and give Annabelle medication, before performing some sort of blood ritual, under the guise of being a doctor at the Tupelo Medical Center. This is a very troubling matter, and one that the police seem to not want to acknowledge."

The room erupted in another wave of murmurs, as everyone turned to look toward the several police officers in the room, who looked around sheepishly.

"Now, according to both Zack and Annabelle, this man was very real, and so was the medicine that he gave to Annabelle. The doctors even verified that the blood that he took from Annabelle's pricked finger, and placed on their foreheads, was real. The strange man, who identified himself as Dr. Luke, even told Zack that Annabelle would live. And, low and behold, the very next morning, she was sitting up on her own, eating again, and had no more pain and fever. How do you explain that?"

"None of us know what exactly transpired that night in Annabelle Owens hospital room, not even Miss Owens and Mr. Calloway. However, what we do know, thanks to the admission of both Annabelle and Zack, that it was not the illicit act of any of her doctors that occurred that night, but a mutual decision, made by two, desperate, love stricken teenagers."

"After Annabelle Owens's miraculous, overnight recovery, Dr. Little and Dr. Brown ordered another round of blood tests, this time for toxicology testing, and sent samples to Birmingham for extensive evaluation. The tests from the local lab showed no signs of any unknown substances in Anna's blood, and the results from Birmingham also showed no signs of poisons, or any other, harmful chemicals. All her x-rays came back clean. By all appearances, Annabelle Owens had been cured."

Mr. Webb moved across the room, until he stood before Anna. "Cured. Annabelle Owens, miraculously, is now cancer free, just days after her doctors told her that she was going to die. Now, I know that many of you will be conflicted by many of the thing that you have heard tonight, but I implore you to ask yourself: Why are we here? Aside from the miraculous healing that occured, and the appearance of the mysterious Dr. Luke, has anything illegal actually occurred here?" More murmurs filled the room, along with a few shrugs, and head nods. Mr. Webb was getting through to them.

"We already know that Dr. Brown was not responsible for the findings of recent sexual activity of Annabelle Owens, but that it was, in fact, a mutual act of love making between a dying girl, and the boy she loves that caused it. Mrs. Owens, a doting, loving mother, had no way of knowing that her weak, sickly daughter would be capable of doing such an act, and was simply acting to fulfil her daughter's dying wish of saying goodbye to her best friend."

"And with that, ladies and gentlemen, I conclude this story. I personally, and wholeheartedly, believe everything that Annabelle Owens and Zack Calloway have told me regarding the events of that night, but now, Annabelle Owens would like to tell you, in her own words, what transpired that night in her hospital room." Mr. Webb motioned for Anna to stand, and with one last, terrified look in my direction, she swallowed, and stood to her feet.

37

Anna Tells Her Story

ANNA STOOD, LOOKING FRAIL and vulnerable. Her eyes were red from crying, and my heart was aching for her. I just wanted to hold her, and to comfort her, but knew she had to do this alone.

"First, before I begin" Anna said, her voice trembling, barely audible, "I want everyone to know how sorry I am for the problems I've caused for Dr. Brown, Dr. Little, and the hospital staff. Also, for the pain I've caused my mother, and Zack's parents. But most of all, to my best friend in this world, Zack Callaway. I never meant to hurt or bring shame to him. You see, I know that I'm only fourteen, but I love Zack Calloway, and when I made the decision to have him spend the night with me, I thought that I was dying."

"The doctors, the nurses, all the people at Tupelo Medical Center could not have been nicer to me," Anna continued. "I loved the doctors who cared for me. I can't explain how I came to be cured of the cancer, but I know that Zack and I both prayed for God to save me, and I believe he heard our prayers. That's the only explanation I have. I know that everything we have told you is true, and I hope that you all will believe what we have said. I invited Zack to my bed, and I fully knew what I was doing. Zack is a good and brave boy, who someday wants to be a doctor himself, right here in Tupelo. Such an injustice could destroy his future, and I know that would break his heart. It would break mine, too."

Anna thanked everyone for listening, and took her seat. Mr. Webb then stood and announced to the room that I would now speak to the group, and tell my side of this unbelievable, surreal story. To say that I was nervous would be hugely understated, but having just watched Anna gave me courage to speak.

"Everything that Anna has told you is true. I don't know what more I can add, but I want to tell you this: I love Annabelle Owens, and would never intentionally do anything to harm her. Like Anna has said, rumors have been flying, some saying Annabelle's mother owns responsibility for allowing me to stay the night in Anna's room. Others have accused Dr. Brown of doing things to Anna. Those rumors are, of course, not true. It was Anna and I who made mistakes. We know that. Mrs. Owens did nothing wrong. If your son or daughter were dying, and there was nothing they could do, wouldn't you do everything in your power to make their final moments special? Could you really deny them the request to say goodbye to someone they love? What would you do?" My voice was as shaky as my nerves, but I started pulling myself together.

"Around Anna's neck she wears a locket," I went on. "A gold locket that I gave her a few months ago. I gave her that locket so that she would remember me forever. She wore that locket the night we made love in the hospital. Anna told me that night that she never went anywhere without the gift that I had given her. She said it was her most valuable possession that she owned, but it wasn't. That night, she gave me the most precious gift that she had to give—her total and complete love. I hope everyone here will not judge Anna, or anyone involved. I know there are some people who will say, "they're fourteen, what do they know about love?" I don't know much, but I believe that love knows nothing about age limits. Our hearts and minds cannot be told to only be in love when you're twenty, or when you're ninety. I believe we come into this world loving. I believe, too, that there is someone special for each of us to love. I believe God meant for me to love Annabelle Owens."

I sat down, and Mr. Webb stood and asked if there were any questions from anyone present. The chief of police turned briefly to the county sheriff, said a few words, and then stood. Mr. Webb looked toward Judge Harper and nodded, and he sat down. The judge recognized the chief.

"Chief, do you have something you would like to say?"

"Yes, your honor, I would. I have conferred with my head detective, who has been looking into this case and with the county sheriff, and we all agree that no charges will be filed against Mr. Zack Calloway or Miss Annabelle Owens," a murmur spread through the room. "As far as the concern for Mrs. Owens's actions, we can see nowhere that she has committed a crime—poor judgement, maybe, but no crime. No charges will be filed in this case. However, any civil action against Mrs. Owens will be left up to the hospital administrator. We will continue to investigate the mysterious doctor that came into the room during the night, though we have no leads yet on this mysterious person who these two say came into the room on the night." The chief took his seat.

Dr. Jonathan Duke, the hospital administrator, stood, and the judge recognized him.

"Dr. Duke, do you have something you would like to add?"

"Just a few words, your honor. Concerning Mrs. Owens, there will be no action taken by the Tupelo Medical Center. The issue is closed. That goes for the accusations against Dr. Brown as well. The hospital will also reimburse all expenses incurred by Mrs. Owens for the time that Annabelle was hospitalized. We feel that is the least we can do, considering it was our staff that made such an incorrect diagnosis of the extent of the cancer. We will, of course, also continue to try to determine who was in the room with Mr. Calloway and Miss Owens." Mr. Duke sat back down.

Judge Harper waited a few second before he spoke again.

"If there's no further discussion, I would like to add this: This case has been resolved, and I believe it was resolved in a fair and reasonable manner. I want to thank you all for your assistance in settling this issue. I believe it would have been a travesty of justice if there had been a different outcome. I will remind everyone in this chamber that what has been stated in this chamber, stays in this chamber. Any discussion outside this courtroom, those persons could well be held in contempt by this court. We do not need anyone more to have their reputations called into question regarding this matter. Do not test my resolve on this matter. This hearing is adjourned."

We descended the steps before the courthouse, and I felt as though the weight of the world had been lifted from my shoulders. Before we separated, Anna took my hand, and smiled brightly.

"Can we sit for a moment?" she asked, gesturing toward a stone bench beneath a large magnolia tree. I nodded, and hollered to Pappy that I would be along soon. He and Momma waved to us, and Anna's mother came over and asked if she was going to ride home with her or walk.

"I'll be home shortly, mother," Anna told her. "Zack will walk me. We have things to talk about before we go."

Anna's mother didn't look thrilled, but she nodded, and walked to her car. Once she was out of sight, Anna kissed me tenderly, and I pulled her close to me, holding her as though it might be for the last time.

"That might be the last kiss you get from me for a while," Anna said sadly. "Just because Judge Harper settled the rumors against us, doesn't mean it's settled with my mother. She may keep me locked up until I'm forty."

"Then, I guess I will have to wait until I'm forty. Should we get one, last milkshake?"

"No. Not until we go and thank Mr. Webb for helping us," Anna said.

We made our way to Mr. Webb's office, where we caught him on the sidewalk with Pete, talking with some people on the street. We stopped and waited until he was finished with his conversation before we approached him. He smiled at us as we approached.

"What a nice surprise to see you two smiling and happy," he said, shaking my hand. "What brings you two over here?"

"We just wanted to come by and say thank you for what you did for us. I don't know what we would have done without your help," I said. "I know Momma and Pappy will come by to thank you, too."

"Oh, that's not necessary," Mr. Webb said. "However, Albert Davis once told me that your momma made some fine chicken and dumplings. Maybe she'll invite me to supper sometime."

"Yes, sir. I think she'd like that."

We said goodbye to Mr. Webb and his grandson, and stopped by the drugstore to grab a couple of milkshakes to take with us. Anna's house was a few blocks from the school, where we would both be starting back in just a few days. At her house, Mrs. Owens was seated on the porch steps, a glass of iced tea in her hand.

"You two want some tea?" she asked as we walked up.

"No, ma'am, we just had a milkshake at the drugstore, and I've got to go. I'm sure Pappy has plenty more to say to me," I said.

"Zack," Mrs. Owens said, "you are welcome to come to see Anna once each week for the time being, and you may call her from time to time. You both are good kids, and do not deserved to be punished any more than you already have, but it's my responsibility to look out for Anna's best interests. I hope you will honor my request."

"I will do that, Mrs. Owens. But Pappy may restrict me more than that, and I will have to do as what he wants. Pappy and Momma like Anna though, and I'm hoping that they won't be too hard on me."

Before I left, Anna wrapped her arms around me in a hug. I held her tightly to my chest, just for a moment, and then we said goodbye. I walked back the way I had come. When I reached the First Presbyterian Church, I stopped and sat for a while on the entrance steps to the old church, prayed, and gave thanks to God for loving me and Anna. It was peaceful and quiet place and I felt very calm and full of happiness despite the troubles of the last few days.

It was well past noon, and the day was hot, but there was a pleasant breeze in the air, and the big elms and white oaks along Jefferson gave plenty of shade until I reached Broadway. From there, I crossed Main Street, went down past the lumber yard, and then on to our house. Somehow, I knew that today was a defining day in mine and Anna's life. Pappy had always said that difficult times, and the way that a person faces them, are what determines a person's character. I didn't know what the future would hold for us, but I knew that whatever it brought, Annabelle Owens would be the person I wanted to share the rest of my life with.

The sun was bright and hot, but the scent of Annabelle Owens was sweet on my chest where I had held her to me. Anna's town of Tupelo was quiet, and I had learned that day that there were plenty of good and fair people there. I had learned to love it as Anna did. Big Flat now seemed like a distant memory. Tupelo was now my home as well. One day, Anna and I would call Tupelo *our* home, and that thought was enough for now.

In the dark shadows of the giant oak trees across from Tupelo's Presbyterian Church, hidden from sight by searching, questioning gazes, Dr. Luke stood and watched as Zack Calloway prayed on the steps of the of the sanctuary. A smile spread across his face, as he turned his eyes toward the cloudless heavens. He nodded his head, as if in approval, and then stepped deeper into the shadows, disappearing without a trace.

Printed in the United States
By Bookmasters